MACKENZIE (A HIDDEN AGENDA)

MacKenzie
(A Hidden Agenda)

MICHAEL HESELTINE

SERENDIPITY

Copyright © Michael Heseltine, 2003

First published in 2003 by
Serendipity
Suite 530
37 Store Street
Bloomsbury
London

The author wishes to state that all persons and events
contained in this book are totally fictitious and
entirely the product of his own imagination;
any resemblance to anyone, alive or dead , is purely coincidental

British Library Cataloguing-in-Publication data
A record for this book is available from the British Library

ISBN 1 84394 052 3

Printed and bound in Europe by the Alden Group, Oxford

To Gerald Heseltine, a loving father who would be proud of this moment

Acknowledgements

To Christine for her support and encouragement

CHAPTER ONE

'Oh for crying out loud. What on earth are we going to do about these?' Peter Maxwell said, throwing down the latest crime figures onto the highly polished table.

The Cabinet meeting was in progress. Peter Maxwell, the current Labour Prime Minister, was in the middle of his second term in office. He had recently had the biggest slating of his political career over the escalating crime figures.

The press were having a field day with headlines such as 'The highest crime figures of any political party this century'. His performance and the development of his party had never been so closely scrutinised.

Peter Maxwell was forty-five years old, a slim fellow, but the last six years since becoming Prime Minister had taken their toll, and he was looking the age of someone far older. He was weary and desperate.

Number 10 Downing Street had consumed many a heated discussion over its long history. The cold white walls of the Cabinet Room were set alight by a highly polished mahogany table, surrounded by men and women of wisdom. Each one of them had their own hidden agenda – all fighting for survival, the right to keep their seat at the table.

The Cabinet Room was humming and it was becoming difficult to know who was saying what, to whom. Wisdom appeared to have gone out of the window when, suddenly, a loud 'bang' overtook the gathering as Maxwell brought his fist down onto the table and rose to his feet.

'Ladies and Gentlemen!' he said, 'The time has come for drastic action to be taken to combat the continual rise of crime in this country.'

He looked across the table at Paul Lomax, the Home Secretary. Paul could see for the first time ever in Maxwell's eyes, how cold and piercing his stare could be. Maxwell began to pace around the room. He knew that if he did not get this issue right, his time at Number 10 would be short-lived. He said, more gently, 'We need to plan and improve our performance people, otherwise we will not be sat in this room for very much longer. I am looking to you Paul, to do something, now! It's your responsibility, so get a grip of the situation. You have six months to show some improvement. Do you understand?'

Lomax replied, 'Yes Prime Minister.'

Lomax rose and left the room.

As he shut the door he could see his career coming to an end. The sound of the door closing appeared to ricochet around the whole hallway of Number 10. His mind was swimming; he could hear his name being ridiculed behind him. He thought to himself, those people, his friends, how could they blame him? What could he alone do? He knew what the problem was. DRUGS, drugs, drugs, drugs, he thought. Theft, burglaries and street robberies are all committed for drug money; everything is to do with drugs.

Lomax returned to Westminster. He couldn't remember the journey from Number 10. Having entered his office and shut the door, he walked to his desk and sat down. It was time for some serious thinking, he said to himself as he gazed at a photograph contained in a silver gilt frame of his wife and children, which stood peering out between the in and out trays on the desk top.

Paul Lomax had begun his political career in 1988 when he

was twenty-five years of age, and a young aspiring Labourite. Born in Hull, he had been raised on the council estates of Preston Road and Longhill. His parents were unemployed, and being the second eldest of a family of five he soon learned the value of not having. He knew the culture of theft, burglary, and the misery it brings. He knew then that drugs were a big problem. Crime was rife, and everyone wanted what the other had. He was sick of it. Paul had a secondary education, and did well gaining several A levels. He attended at Hull University where he obtained a First Class Honours Degree in History and Politics.

Following in the footsteps of the local East Hull MP, John Prescott, he joined the local Labour Group where he became hungry for power. It was there he decided his goal was to become a Member of Parliament. He found his road to fame hard and long. After serving a period on the local Council, he became an MP seven years later and gained a seat in the Cabinet within two years, during Maxwell's reshuffle in his first term of office.

Lomax still in his office, thought, 'Where did it all begin? Was it the lack of parental control? Perhaps the lack of discipline throughout school life? No one had any respect for people or property. What they can't have, they take. What a shit world we're in! Well it's up to me. What can I do?' He thought long and hard.

Suddenly, Lomax's attention was distracted by the sound of the telephone ringing. He answered it.

'Hello darling, are you coming home today?' Lomax realised that the sweet sound was that of his wife, Lorraine. He again looked at the photograph.

Paul said, 'Sorry dear, what time is it?'

On saying this, he glanced at the clock standing on the mantel over the fireplace in his office. He hadn't realised that the hours had flown by and that it was eight in the evening. 'Sorry darling. I'll be leaving shortly.'

He rose from his desk, turned off the table light and left the office. It was a strange evening. His mind was really not focusing on anything. He arrived home and was greeted with a kiss on the cheek from Lorraine and a cuddle from the children, James and Samantha. He ate a delightful meal, prepared and gracefully served by his wife. A meal of salmon fillets, potatoes, peas and carrots all dressed in a superb Hollandaise sauce, flushed down with a chilled glass of dry white wine.

'Was it a good day at the office darling?' Lorraine asked.

Paul ignored her at first, but when she repeated the question he replied, 'Crap.'

'Oh dear,' she said and rose from her seat to begin clearing the dinner table.

Paul spent the rest of the evening roaming from one thing to another. He couldn't settle to anything. He went to bed but couldn't sleep and as he listened to the sound of Lorraine gently snoring next to him, he got out of bed and stood looking out of the bedroom window. The sky was clear and the stars shone bright. 'Yes!' he said. Paul had thought of a solution.

An idea, which he recalled, in Maxwell's own words, was 'drastic action'. It was an idea that if executed well, would go down in history as the crime of the century. The question was how not to get caught.

The next morning Paul rose at eight a.m., washed, showered and skipped breakfast. He kissed the kids goodbye and shouted to Lorraine, 'See you later darling.'

Lorraine replied, 'Don't forget the dinner engagement tonight darling.' There was no answer. 'Paul?' she shouted. Paul had left without making a reply. Lorraine glanced out of the window and could see Paul's car pulling out of the driveway on to the main road.

Paul entered his office and pressed the button on his intercom, 'Helen, can I see you please?'

Helen Phillips had been a ministerial secretary for twenty-three years having served under many a Home Secretary. She was a faithful and trustworthy member of staff. Paul looked at her, thinking to himself, 'By, you must have been a stunner in your younger days. You still have that something about you.'

He said, 'Helen, cancel all my meetings and appointments for the next four days.'

'Are you sure?' she questioned. 'You have some very important meetings coming up.'

Paul replied sternly, 'Yes, I wouldn't have said so if I wasn't sure. There is nothing that cannot be rescheduled. Can I borrow your laptop computer as well?'

Helen looked a little surprised by this request and said, 'Yes, of course.'

She returned to her desk, disconnected the laptop and handed it to Paul.

'Don't disturb me for the next few hours,' he said. He sat down at his desk, connected the laptop and began tapping away at the keys.

Helen wondered what on earth was going on. This was not like Paul. She paused for a while, then started to cancel everything in the diary for the next four days. Paul appeared some three hours later saying, 'I'm going out for a while. Do not under any circumstances touch or allow anyone else to touch the computer.'

Helen replied, 'Yes Sir,' a little sarcastically.

Paul left the building without saying where he was going. Over the next two days he had unscheduled meetings with the Commissioner of the Metropolitan Police, Sir Michael Collins. They had agreed that more effort should be put into dealing with the country's drug problem and that any proposals should be implemented straight away. Sir Michael was to contact all Chief Officers of Police on leaving the meeting.

The next meeting was with Commander Kenneth Jones who had control of the drugs section under the direction of Customs and Excise. Helen was not allowed to attend this meeting which was unusual, and she felt as if she had had her nose put out of place.

The third meeting was with a man who gave the name Major Christopher Parker, retired. Helen wondered why Paul Lomax should be having a meeting with a retired Major. Maybe he was an old friend of Paul's, but he didn't seem old enough for that, she thought. He'd not mentioned the name Christopher Parker before.

Parker appeared to be younger than Paul. He had a very muscular build to him, with short cut, dark hair with greying tinges to it. He stood bolt upright and was very confident and strode around the office as if he owned the place.

Helen chuckled at one point when the Major tripped over a fraying piece of carpet when he was trying to appear so prim and proper. He glanced round the room to see if she was watching. Paul's office intercom sounded and a request was made to send the Major through to see Paul. Helen stood up and said, 'This way Major' and showed the Major into the office.

'Major Christopher Parker, ' she announced in a posh accent, slightly mimicking the Major's confident attitude.

'Thank you Helen. That's all for now. You may leave,' Paul said.

Again Helen was annoyed. She couldn't understand why she was being kept out of these meetings. She always took the minutes of meetings. Two and a half hours later Paul's office door opened and Helen heard Paul saying to the Major, 'Remember, use the telephone number I've given you. Speak to me only if you need to, and this meeting has not taken place.'

Paul walked out of the office with the Major who was holding onto an A4 folder marked with the words 'FOR YOUR EYES ONLY'. Helen thought to herself that the Major didn't have that with him when he entered, so Paul must have given it to him. She wondered what it contained.

As the Major left, Paul had a grin on his face for the first time in days. 'Time for coffee I think, Helen.'

After coffee Paul requested Helen to contact the Prime Minister's office and arrange a meeting with Maxwell. At three thirty p.m. the following day Maxwell granted a five-minute hearing with Paul after parliamentary question time. Paul knew from this that Maxwell had visions to replace him from office at the earliest opportunity.

Behind closed doors Maxwell said to Paul, 'Yes, what can I do for you?'

Paul stated that he had commenced measures that he hoped would suddenly and effectively solve the crime problem. 'Do you want to know what measures I've implemented?' Paul added.

Sharply Maxwell replied, 'No, do whatever you need to do, you don't have another chance.'

The meeting closed. Neither knew the full consequences that were to follow.

Paul left the Houses of Parliament. As he walked down the steps, the sun was shining, and he looked back at the magnificent grandeur of the building and thought what history unfolds within the confines of these walls. What has been put in place cannot be stopped. He paused, glanced back down the steps and watched the grey pigeons scrambling for scraps on the pavement; a black moment went through his mind.

That could be me.

CHAPTER TWO

The Royal Courts of Justice stand proudly on The Strand, London, WC2 2LL. Within the stone-clad walls of this fine old building there had been heard many a trial. Men and women had been sentenced to hang by the neck, until they died.

IRA bombers had been sentenced to numerous life sentences.

Here am I, Chief Inspector Alan Duncan MacKenzie, doing my little bit to make Britain a safer place.

MacKenzie was deep in thought and his mind was imagining what times may have been like in the old days, when the judge sat in his purple robe and red sash, his wig looking as if it needed a damn good wash, when at the end of a trial the black cap was placed onto his head. Then he would look at some poor old fellow in the dock who knew what the next words were going to be. 'You have been found guilty of the most horrendous crime against man, that of murder. I sentence you to be taken from here to a place of execution where you will hang until you are ...'

At that point MacKenzie's Sergeant, Frank Butcher, gave him a nudge with his elbow. The slightly startled MacKenzie sat bolt upright trying not to show that he was away, in some far off world of his own, not listening to what was happening in court.

The Judge, the Right Honourable Mr Justice Barber had just completed his summing up of the case. MacKenzie heard him say, 'Members of the Jury, I am now going to send you out so you can consider your deliberations on this case. However, if you feel the need to come back to this court to ask any questions, feel free to do so. You may now go with the Usher.'

The jury left the courtroom. The Judge made some cryptic comment to the Barristers who felt obliged to laugh. The court rose and he left. MacKenzie said to Butcher, 'Lunch then,' and off they went to the Elephant and Castle for a sandwich and a pint.

MacKenzie, a Scot born in Aberdeen on the East Coast of Scotland, was forty-nine years of age, having only spent the first ten years of his life north of the border. His family moved to the 'big city' of London due to his father's work.

His father was a ship engineer and served during the war in submarines. On returning to Aberdeen the years had taken their toll on the marine industry. Closures began at the shipyards and MacKenzie Senior took the decision to move to London. MacKenzie Senior had hoped that his son Alan would continue the line of family engineers and follow in his father's footsteps. Alan had other intentions.

Alan Duncan MacKenzie had a basic education in London schools, leaving at the age of sixteen. Fortunately for him, by leaving Scotland early he managed to shed his broad Scottish accent. He gained four O Levels in English literature, maths, general studies and biology.

Alan brushed off the engineering tradition and joined the Metropolitan Police as a Police cadet. After three years as a cadet he was sworn in as a Constable and began pounding the beat in Hammersmith. He didn't take the accelerated promotion route but eventually climbed to the rank of Chief Inspector by merit and sheer hard work. He found the rise upward through the ranks long and tiresome. His pet hate was his colleagues who had succeeded via the accelerated promotion procedure, now trying to run the Police Service without having done any policing on the street, and who in his view, were making a right damn mess of it all. Alan believed the rise to power and influence should be earned, and not given.

Alan was a married man with no children. He had been married fifteen years and his hatred for his accelerated promoted colleagues was heightened when his wife recently left him for a younger Superintendent in the traffic division. His divorce had just been finalised and he now appeared to be spending even more of his time at work. His only problem now was that he expected that everyone who worked under him should also work as many hours.

At 4 p.m. that day the jury was recalled into the court. An eerie silence becalmed the court as Mr Justice Barber said, 'Have you reached a verdict?'

As he spoke, an extremely thin young woman rose from her seat. She looked at the Judge, bent her head slightly as she peered over her dark rimmed spectacles and said quietly, 'No your Honour.'

Alan thought, 'Good god, talk about the wheels of justice grinding to a halt. What on earth have they got to think about? He's guilty.'

The Judge, after asking the jury if they needed more time to deliberate or whether they were in deadlock, stood the jury down until 10 a.m. the following morning.

On leaving the court the two Police Officers found it to be raining and as Sergeant Butcher put his raincoat on, Alan stated that he would be late in the morning because he had some paperwork to clear in the office.

On parting he said to Frank, 'If there's a problem ring me.'

Alan set off walking along The Strand and as he hadn't brought a coat, decided to call into a nearby café and grab a cup of coffee whilst it stopped raining.

As he sat, the door to the café burst open. Alan's attention was suddenly pointed in that direction only to see falling onto the floor into a heap, the figure of a woman. He jumped to his feet and went to assist the woman. 'Oh dear,' he said, 'Can I help you?'

The woman had something about her, he thought to himself. About forty-two, maybe forty-three years of age, five foot nine inches tall of slim build. She had collar-length, mousy brown coloured hair and smelt passionately of Yves Saint Laurent Opium perfume. He could tell that she still kept a neat figure hidden under the expensive, but crumpled clothing she wore.

She said, 'I seem to have tripped over the doorstep in my rush to get out of the rain.'

She began rubbing the lower half of her left leg and stated that she felt she had twisted it. Alan, after asking if he might examine her leg, gave it the once over and said that no permanent damage had been done. He assisted her to her feet and sat her down at his table.

'Coffee?' he said. 'I don't mind if I do,' she replied. After introducing themselves they had coffee and chatted about the mishaps in life. Alan became slightly annoyed as the café owner kept interrupting their conversation, fussing over his new companion. He was quite taken aback by the good-looking woman who confronted him and on learning that she was unattached decided to escort her home, sharing a taxi.

'It's very kind of you to allow me to share your taxi,' she said.

'Not at all, don't even think about it,' he replied.

The taxi pulled up outside a block of Georgian apartments not far from Leicester Square. Alan asked the taxi driver to wait, whilst he saw that she was safe and well to her front door. He gazed for a moment pondering his next move and found himself for a short period observing the large black painted front door with its ornate, larger than life brass knocker beneath the number 15 that shone proudly from the centre bar.

He built up the courage to say, 'Look, I'm by myself, would you like to go out with me sometime?' He sounded very nervous and she replied, without hesitation, 'Yes, When?'

They agreed to meet the following Friday night at a popular restaurant called 'The White Rose', not far from where she lived. Alan returned to the taxi, and as he got to the door he looked back and smiled, gave a quick wave and climbed into the back seat. 'Isle of Dogs please,' he shouted to the driver.

The taxi stopped outside a large block of modern flats built within the last three years. The entrance to the flats was illuminated, almost as if a dozen searchlights had been turned on. Alan paid the driver, 'Cheers Guv,' he said as he was told to keep the change. The taxi drove away and disappeared into the evening traffic, which had begun to build up on the main road.

Alan entered his flat, put the kettle on and began to run a bath. He was tired, having spent the last sixteen months heading a team investigating the murder of a prostitute. The job was coming to a close. He pondered for a while thinking about the day, the moment in the café and having met an attractive woman, by chance. If it hadn't been raining, he would probably be spending Friday night in alone. A wry smile came on his face. Maybe, he thought, my luck is about to change.

The next morning Alan turned up at the Court around eleven thirty. Having spoken to Frank, he disappeared to liaise with the Prosecuting Counsel, who assured Alan that there was nothing to worry about and that the trial had gone according to plan.

At three fifteen that afternoon the jury entered the court to return its verdict. Again an eerie silence fell upon the court. You could almost hear a pin drop as both sides, Defence and Prosecution, waited for the lady foreperson to speak. She rose to her feet and cleared her throat. Time seemed endless, then the words came, 'Guilty your Honour.'

The Right Honourable Justice Barber paused. As he did so, shouts came out of the public gallery, 'Bastards!' It was obvious to all present in the court that the family of the accused was not happy with the verdict.

The Judge shouted to all gathered therein, 'Silence, I will not put up with such an outburst.'

MacKenzie looked at Frank Butcher and whispered, 'Sergeant, wait until we get out of court before you smile.'

At that point the Judge looked towards the accused, Peter Worth, and said, 'You have been found guilty of the most horrendous crime against man, that of murder.' On hearing this Alan chuckled to himself, recalling his earlier thought about the old days.

The Judge continued, 'I sentence you to Life imprisonment. Take him down.'

The Judge thanked the Barristers for their attention in the case and then promptly offered a commendation to the Police Officers who conducted the enquiry. The court rose and the Judge departed. Alan crossed the courtroom floor and thanked the Barrister for a job well done. He then turned to Frank, took his right hand and shook it saying, 'Well done.' They then both left the court.

Detective Chief Inspector Alan Duncan MacKenzie and Detective Sergeant Frank Butcher returned to the incident room at New Scotland Yard to a round of applause. The result of the case had already filtered back to the enquiry team. Alan shouted out and the room became silent, 'Well what can I say, the end product is all down to you. Thank you for your hard work and devotion and I hope I'll have the opportunity to work with you again. I believe there's a do arranged at The Old Bill Pub later.' MacKenzie then produced a large bottle of Teachers malt from the top drawer of his desk and said 'This will set you off in the party mood.'

The week went quickly by and Friday night approached. Alan managed to get away from work earlier than usual. He had been thinking of ways in which he could make the night special. He had forgotten the courting ways, as it was a long time since he had dated anyone. Okay, he knew flowers and chocolates were still a good idea, but what were the modern methods of courtship? He felt foolish having these thoughts going through his mind. It was like being a teenager again.

MacKenzie thought the evening was fated from the start having spilt a calming glass of red wine down his suit trousers and then pulling a button off his only ironed shirt. With ironing board out, he quickly steam pressed a clean shirt, however when he put it on he thought it looked as though it had been pressed under the bed mattress. His efforts had been in vain.

The normally confident MacKenzie left his flat at 7.30 p.m. He felt nervous about the encounter he was due to have with the lovely woman he had met earlier in the week. Then he was sitting in the taxi and as it approached The White Rose restaurant he again felt like that teenager about to meet a girl for the first time ever. 'Oh god, stop it,' he whispered to himself.

The taxi driver, being a typical Londoner, tried his best to make conversation with Alan. 'Are you alright Guv?' he asked.

'Sorry?' Alan replied. The taxi driver went straight back into talk mode, oblivious to the fact that his passenger was taking no notice of him. Alan was away into a world of his own.

The taxi pulled up outside the restaurant. 'That's four pounds fifty Guv please,' the driver said. Alan handed over a crisp five-pound note and told the taxi driver to keep the change. Without a second thought the driver placed the taxi into first gear and commenced to drive off, shouting to Alan 'Thanks Guv, have a good night.'

Alan walked into the pub and approached the bar where he ordered a large gin and tonic from the barmaid. 'Phew', he thought to himself as he tried not to notice that the young girl behind the bar was wearing a short skirt and low cut top. He scanned the premises from back to front. On not seeing anybody he recognised he glanced at his watch and wondered if his date for the evening was going to turn up.

A few minutes elapsed when, without warning, Alan was tapped gently on the shoulder. 'Hello,' a voice said, 'I hope you're not eyeing that young woman up?'

Alan turned his head and saw the figure of a beautiful woman. She had immaculate make up, and Alan could smell the distinctive aroma of Yves Saint Laurent Opium perfume. 'Hi,' he said. 'May I get you a drink?'

The attractive woman ordered a glass of red wine and the two of them went to take their place at the table. The table was set, dressed in pink napkins and matching petite pink flowers which seem to protrude from an under-sized vase. They ordered food and a bottle of Cabernet Sauvignon 1997. A three-course meal was served and consumed with complete eloquence and two hours later the table was cleared.

'Shall we go into the lounge for a while?' Alan suggested, hoping that she would say yes. He wasn't sure if he had bored her with the conversations about police work and the state of the country.

She replied, 'Yes,' and they both left the dining room. They found a couple of empty chairs near to the window, which overlooked the rear gardens of the restaurant. The evening flew by and it appeared that both of them were enjoying the company.

Closing time loomed and Alan ordered a taxi. It arrived quickly as if it had been parked round the corner, they both got in and the taxi began to drive away. Alan was disappointed that the evening was drawing to a close; he didn't want it to end. He hadn't relaxed so much for such a long time.

The taxi slowed to a halt outside number 15 St Catherine's Court. The row of Georgian houses was dimly lit with black cast-iron lampposts which had originally been illuminated by gas, but were now converted to electricity. They both got out of the taxi. 'I have had a wonderful evening,' she quietly whispered to Alan. 'Send the taxi away, and come in for a coffee.'

Alan did not require a second request and duly paid the taxi driver. As the taxi drove off, the large black door closed with a quiet echo that broke the still night air.

CHAPTER THREE

Major Christopher Parker joined the Parachute Regiment on the 20th January 1972. On completing his initial training, he was identified by the military top brass as a shining light and was singled out. He was destined for higher things. After passing his induction course he joined the famous 3rd Parachute Regiment. He knew that the regiment was steeped in history and he wanted to be part of it.

After a year, Parker was seconded to special training in which he seemed to excel beyond everyone's expectations. He was transferred from the regiment to the Special Air Services, the so-called elite of the British Army.

Major Parker was known as 'Olly' to his close friends. He was given the nickname early in his career because his facial appearance resembled that of an owl. He had thick eyebrows and square face and his ears were slightly pointed. He wore a moustache neatly trimmed. His mates used to take the Mickey saying that he must have spent hours in front of the mirror trimming it. The Major gave the appearance of being meek and mild, but beneath that soft exterior was a man as hard as nails.

Parker had once been held captive behind enemy lines whilst engaged on a mission in Columbia. Having spent the longest fortnight of his life being interrogated, he was rescued in a dawn raid on the encampment where he was being held hostage. It was later discovered that his interrogators even failed to get his name and unit number. However the encounter was believed to be his downfall as his head never really recovered from the ordeal.

Due to his age, although he was only thirty-nine, he was increasingly finding it difficult to keep up with the new blood in the regiment. 'They', the top brass, took the decision to take Parker out of operational duties and put him as a training instructor. From that point the Major's mental problems began to take hold and some of his decisions were rash and uncompromising. The final push came for Parker, which led to his resignation from the Army, when he took recruits for jungle training exercises. He put himself and his men at risk of losing their lives. The subsequent enquiry clearly slated Parker and criticised him for his bad judgements.

The man was wounded in the heart and after a career where he received the Military Cross for Gallantry and three Citations for Bravery, he was required to resign. He entered 'Civvi Street' disgruntled and feeling that the government owed him something. He ended up like a lot of trained killers, fighting as a mercenary for whatever cause paid him the most for his services.

Parker disappeared for a while until the authorities became aware that he was engaged as a mercenary in South America in the recent Argentinean political uprisings. When he returned to the UK, the meeting with Lomax was like a breath of fresh air to him and he believed, in his own mind, that at last they were putting things right. The price tag for the job Lomax offered was too inviting.

Major Christopher Parker MC, retired did not know that Lomax had earmarked him as the scapegoat if the wheel came off, if Lomax's plans went wrong.

As a result of his meeting with Lomax, Chris Parker had been busy. He had opened the 'For Your Eyes Only' file time and time again, digesting the plans and information it provided. He had to plan and organise his men in four weeks and to carry out the operation within eight weeks. His drive to complete the plan was the sixty to seventy million pounds he was to gain if the plan succeeded.

Lomax, who had dreamed up the plan, waited in anticipation, and as meeting after meeting went on, he chuckled to himself thinking the best part of his plan was that it would cost the government nothing, not a penny. He was wrong – the plan was going to affect his party and the government dearly. Lomax in his desperation had lost sight of the ideals of his country and placed his own self-interests before others.

The file, which had been given to Parker, was full of information. However Parker did not notice that the papers contained in it gave no indication where it had come from or who had compiled it. Lomax's signature appeared nowhere. With such a high price being paid for the job, Parker was able to hire twenty of the best that the army, in their wisdom, had decided to dispense with. He had offered them one million pounds each for the job.

The first person he employed was Paul Evans who was a master tactician and operational planner. Parker paid highly for him, four million. The two of them spent the first three weeks, a time limit Parker had set, together, day and night assessing locations and working out how to execute the operation, and most of all, how to get away with it.

The whole team assembled at the end of the third week. The location Chris had picked for the meeting was a disused farm in Norfolk. Parker addressed the meeting and gave details of the plan that the assembled gathering needed to know. Following the meeting the group went their separate ways as indicated by their instructions.

The group reassembled every two days for training purposes. After a few of these, Parker turned to Evans and said, 'Well

Paul, we are soon to find out whether these past few weeks of preparation will work.'

Evans replied confidently, 'They will, Sir. No problem.'

Parker was alone in a dirty old outbuilding in the farm. He pressed the digits on his mobile phone. It rang. 'Lomax?' he said, 'We're ready.'

Parker ended the call by the word, 'Shit'; the Operation had been postponed for a week.

Preparations ended at 18.30 hours on Saturday 28 November, five weeks to the date of that first meeting with Lomax. Parker for the second time pressed the digits on his mobile 07979 488210. It rang three times. 'Lomax, it's Parker,' he said.

Lomax said little; 'Operation on, expected 05.00 hours tomorrow, repeat 05.00 29–11. Good luck.' The phone went dead.

At 03.00 hours the following day, the assembled team zeroed their watches in true army fashion and set off to their allotted meeting points.

In the cool night air the sound of a crackled radio blurted out, 'Hotel X-ray two one to XH.' 'Hotel X-ray two one go ahead,' it replied.

The Metropolitan Police firearm team were in place, Inspector Tony Mason was in charge. His team were lying in wait at various points around a vehicle dismantlers' yard on the London dockland.

The operation was the conclusion to an eighteen month long investigation by the Customs and Excise Officers, who were also positioned around the yard. This posed a particular problem to Inspector Mason and his team regarding the safety of those involved.

For the past eighteen months Customs Officers had been tracking a large consignment of drugs, heroin, which had been stashed in a forty-ton container. The trail of the drugs ended up in Dobson's Breakers yard which was situated on Foster Street in the heart of London's dockland.

It was expected that the drug dealers were to pick up the consignment at 05.00 hours that morning. The team waited as silence fell around the yard. It was a cool, crisp, frosty morning and a fine mist covered the yard. An eerie haze shone from the streetlights. The still calm was interrupted by the sound of motor vehicles approaching.

Inspector Mason went on his radio, 'Hotel X-ray two one.' 'Go ahead,' was the reply.

'All officers to stand by. We have movement,' he said.

As he observed, he could see a convoy of three vehicles pull to a stop outside the gate to the yard; a 4 x 4 off-road vehicle, a forty-ton tractor unit and a transit van.

A further radio message interrupted Mason's attention, 'Eight persons in all, Sir, four in the 4 x 4, one in the unit and three in the transit van.' The radio crackled. Mason thought to himself, 'Blast. Not radio problems! It must be the atmospherics.' He went on the air again, 'Radio silence until further notice.'

A man got out of the front vehicle and began to unlock the gates; a clanging of chains could clearly be heard. The gates opened and the man returned to his vehicle and slammed his door shut.

The convoy of vehicles drove into the yard. The two escorting vehicles came to a halt and the tractor unit began to reverse towards the container trailer. Seven men got out of the vehicles and formed a cordon around the container. They were armed. The gears of the 'artic' crunched as if the driver was having problems getting it into gear. It started to reverse. The vehicle suddenly jolted to a halt as the coupling of the tractor unit met the trailer.

Over the radio the words, 'Go. Go. Go,' sounded. The police sprang into action and the drug dealers were surrounded.

Inspector Mason shouted over a loud hailer, 'Armed Police. Stay where you are and lay your weapons on the ground.'

It was obvious to the drug gang that any opposition would be futile and they began to comply with instructions. They lay on the floor and the police moved in. One by one the criminals were arrested, placed into handcuffs and led away into police vehicles, which had now arrived.

Fifteen minutes later it was all over, the firearm team was stood down and they began to place their weapons away.

Parker had been observing the police operation. He thought to himself how smoothly the police had operated and so quickly. His eyebrows raised slightly and he muttered under his breath, 'I hope mine goes as well'.

Parker glanced down at his arm, pulled his sleeve and looked at his watch, it read 05.27 hours. He pressed the button on his radio and instructed his team to move in.

Suddenly, Inspector Mason looked up and said, 'What the hell!' As he did so he could see vehicles racing at speed into the yard. At the same time loud horrendous bangs thundered around the yard causing everyone to fall to the ground. Flashes of light appeared as if a lightning storm had just started.

In moments, four armoured jeeps screeched to a stop; gravel from the surface of the yard sprayed from the wheels like jets of water from a shower. Suddenly Mason heard the sound of automatic fire. He noticed the familiar sound of bullets ricocheting off the compound surface close to him.

A voice hailed from the vehicles, 'Do not resist and no one will get hurt. Do exactly what you are told.'

Mason knew that they and the Customs Officers had been taken by surprise and were helpless. He instructed his men to do as they were told.

A voice shouted out, 'Remain face down on the ground, my men are covering you. Any movement will be met with severe force.'

Mason couldn't believe what was happening and wondered to himself how he managed to get into this hopeless situation, a situation which left him and his team having to comply with a bunch of criminals' instructions.

A few moments had gone by before the articulated vehicle towing the container unit sprang into life and began to pull away from the corner of the yard where it had remained stationary for the past week. Mason saw it being driven out of the yard.

Parker shouted to his men, 'Phase two.' With military precision, members of Parker's team began collecting radios from the Police Officers and Customs officials – they were placed into a nearby police transit van, which was parked in the yard.

Twenty minutes had elapsed since the 'artic' had left the yard. Parker shouted out, 'Phase three.'

At the same time another burst of automatic gunfire disrupted the morning air. Mason glanced round and could see that the gunfire was directed at the police vehicle tyres as each one exploded and burst.

Three of the jeeps began to move off at speed. The other remained. A voice shouted out, 'You will remain here for a further fifteen minutes before you move, if you move before then someone will get hurt.'

The last remaining jeep then drove away. Shortly afterwards, two of the Customs officials began to move, they stood up. Immediately as they did so, the sound of a huge explosion shattered the quiet morning's peace and the force blasted the Customs men into the air causing them to fall heavily to the ground.

Inspector Mason then shouted, 'Stay where you are, we are

obviously being watched.' What Mason didn't know was that the vehicle had been fitted with a movement detector, set to explode if anyone moved in the yard. Parker had planned this to happen anyway in order to get rid of the police radios, which had been placed into the van.

Ten minutes later a further explosion occurred which appeared to come from all around the yard and at the same time a bright flash of light lit the whole yard. Parker had set a second set of thunder flashes to detonate in order to allow his team valuable time to escape.

In the distance could be heard the sound of sirens. A few minutes later Mason was relieved to see blue flashing lights enter the breaker's yard as he saw police, fire and ambulances arrive.

Mason stood up and thought to himself, 'How do I explain this one away to the boss?' He gazed at the firemen putting the fire out on the burning police vehicle. He checked his men who were safe and well and then checked the Customs men who were injured but not seriously.

An immediate search was organised for the container vehicle and the persons responsible for the theft of it. As daylight broke, the breaker's yard was cordoned off and Scenes of Crime Officers were busy combing the area for evidence.

The Force Helicopter Unit made an aerial search, but as time went by the Customs officers realised that the consignment of drugs was lost. The tracking device which had been on the container had failed due to the battery being flat. It had not been replaced when the container was parked in the yard as it was thought observations would be a better course of practice.

Within hours recriminations started flowing between the Customs and Police as to who was at fault.

CHAPTER FOUR

At 7.20 a.m. the same morning the mobile telephone rang. 'MacKenzie' he answered. All he said then was, 'Where? When? How? I'll be in shortly.'

By 8.15 a.m. MacKenzie was at Scotland Yard and in his office. He was met by Frank Butcher who said, 'All hell's let loose in here, boss.'

MacKenzie spent the next few hours being brought up to date on the night's events and arranging to visit the scene. Before leaving the office he told the office manager to arrange a full briefing at 11.30. He left instructions that all interested parties were to be present at the briefing.

At 10.30 a.m. the telephone rang. Parker, full of confidence after obtaining his objective, said, 'Lomax?'

It answered, 'Yes.'

'Parker here. Part one of the operation successfully completed, part two to commence.'

The voice replied, 'Very well.' Lomax switched his phone off. Parker's mobile went dead.

Lomax was sitting at his desk in his office. On receiving the telephone call he placed his head in his hands and let out a deep breath. At that time his office door opened and Helen entered. 'Are you alright Paul?' she asked.

Lomax replied, 'Yes thank you, but have you got any headache tablets, my head's splitting.'

Helen replied, 'Yes I think so.' She then left the office for a short time and returned holding two paracetamol tablets in her hand. She handed them to Paul dropping them gently into his hand.

Helen then went through the diary for the day with Paul and then left the office. Paul pondered for a while and wondered if he should call the whole idea off. 'No it's too late for that,' he said to himself. 'May the devil take its course.'

There was a feeling of jubilation at the old farm, the operation had gone well and Parker's boys were celebrating. Parker shouted out, 'Lads it's not finished yet, we still have to sell this lot to the drug dealers. Then with a million in your hand, you'll have cause to celebrate.' A loud yell sounded around the barn where they had gathered. Parker then set part two of the operation into motion.

Parker watched as each of his men were dressed in white overalls and wearing masks, gloves and goggles.

The drugs were unloaded from the container, then each bag was emptied and mixed with another substance provided by Parker. The drugs were being broken down with another agent. This would be undetectable by the drug dealers to whom it was to be sold.

The gathered mixture of military off-loads did not question Parker's motive for anything they were doing. They had a job to do and would carry out their orders without blinking an eye. They were unaware of what substance they were mixing with the heroin, only that at all times they were to wear the protective clothing provided by Parker. They were of the opinion that it was to protect them from the effects of heroin.

None of them knew who was to protect them from Parker.

* * *

Lomax's headache failed to clear and at mid afternoon he called Helen into the office and said, 'I'm going home.'

Helen said enquiringly, 'Oh that's not like you Paul. What's wrong?'

Paul quietly replied, 'You don't want to know.'

Helen smiled and with a slight laughter in her voice said, 'Well if it's to do with Maxwell, I wouldn't worry, his bark's worse than his bite.'

Paul left the office and climbed into his silver Jaguar and drove off into the London traffic. He pondered and thought, he wasn't sure if his headache was as a result of the events surrounding Parker, stress over the fact that he might lose his job shortly, or worry over the next stage of the plan. Paul was now helpless to stop the operation. He felt that to cancel now would invoke Parker's revenge, a revenge, which he felt, would be upon him.

Before leaving the office Helen took the opportunity to make a telephone call. On the phone being answered she said, 'Hi, it's only me. I wondered if we were going to be doing anything tonight?'

Helen received a reply, 'Err yes, but I don't know what time I'll get away, I'll ring you later.'

'OK,' she replied. She put the phone down and began rummaging through the papers Paul had chucked into her tray on leaving the office.

Lorraine Lomax was sat at home when she glanced out of the lounge window and saw Paul's car travelling down the drive. She got up and walked into the hallway just at the time when she could hear the gravel crunching on the drive as Paul's car came to a stop.

Paul opened the front door and was greeted by Lorraine saying, 'Good heavens what's the matter with you?'

'Don't start Lorraine, I can't be bothered with your stupid quips,' he blurted back. He walked into the lounge, approached the drinks cabinet and poured himself a double brandy. Then he suggested to Lorraine that when the children came home from school that they should go out for tea and maybe take them to the cinema or to the bowling alley.

Lorraine replied to this suggestion with surprise, 'By, you must be ill if you want to take the kids out.'

Paul gulped the brandy down in one go. 'Don't you ever stop going on?' he shouted. He walked off and said, 'I'm off for a shower,' slamming the door behind him.

James and Samantha returned home from school and they were just as amazed as Lorraine when Paul suggested that they go out. The two children then started squabbling with each other as to where they would like to go.

A venue was decided and after going to McDonald's for tea they went ten-pin bowling. They arrived at the Mecca bowling alley at around 7.30 p.m. that evening.

* * *

A few hours earlier Alan MacKenzie had ended his day. It had been busy from the moment he received his early morning telephone call. He had visited the breaker's yard where the robbery had taken place that day and the rest of the day was spent attending meeting after meeting. The 11.30 briefing was the best. When Alan entered the conference room there was pandemonium. Customs and Excise were placing the blame on the police for breach of confidence and the police were blaming them for the same.

Alan shouted out, 'This is not going to help.' The volume of sound in the room came to a whisper.

'I am Alan MacKenzie, Chief Inspector and I have been appointed to take over this investigation.' he said.

He continued by saying that the team of criminals who stole the container shipment was highly trained and professional in the manner in which they carried out the raid at the yard. 'I would like each organisation and department to let us know what their involvement was in this operation, I think we'll start with Customs,' he said as he sat down.

Customs Officer Michael Heritage took the floor and outlined the investigation from the beginning. He told the gathering about the route taken from South America to the Continent where the consignment made its way to Britain and eventually ended up in the breaker's yard in London's dockland.

Heritage then gave the floor over to Customs Officer Charlie Wilson who outlined who the main drug dealers were. He ended up by saying, 'These are the persons that we have in custody now.'

Inspector Mason then took the floor. The gathered group ridiculed him a little before he spoke. MacKenzie said, 'We will have less of that now. It would appear that we all failed to see this other party of villains being involved.'

The gathering again went quiet and Mason began his version of events. He ended by saying, 'No one was more surprised than me as to what happened next.' He then went on to explain why he had stood his team down and how swiftly the offending parties arrived at the scene.

MacKenzie then stood up and said, 'It is obvious what we have got ahead of us. We don't have any leads so we're starting from scratch. Each and everyone involved in today's operation – I want statements before you go off today. I want to see each group inspector in my office in half an hour.'

The meeting closed with a buzz of excitement. Suddenly MacKenzie shouted out, 'Oh by the way, the press have got hold of this, so please keep your mouths shut. I don't want anything leaking from here.'

Frank Butcher handed MacKenzie a freshly brewed mug of tea just as he was about to pick up the telephone. 'Thanks Frank,' he said. MacKenzie started to dial. The ring tone sounded eight times and he was about to put the phone down, when it was answered, 'Hello, it's me,' he said.

'Hi,' the reply came in a calm sexy voice.

'Shall I see you about 7 p.m.?' he asked.

'Yes, if you can get away,' she said.

MacKenzie replied, 'I'll pick you up about seven, do you fancy bowling?'

She laughed and said, 'I haven't done that in years, yes it'll be fun.'

The telephone went dead. MacKenzie thought to himself and passed a few stolen seconds thinking about this woman who he had fallen in love with.

Frank Butcher coughed as he cleared his throat, and said, 'I think, Sir, that we should decide which team is looking at what line of enquiry.'

MacKenzie suddenly burst into life again, placing his work head into motion. Over the next twenty minutes he planned all the lines of enquiry that his teams were going to conduct. He had just finished when a knock on the door broke his thoughts and the enquiry team Inspectors entered the room.

His secretary followed the Inspectors into the office and shouted to him, 'You have to see the Commissioner in the morning at 11 a.m.' She then closed the door.

MacKenzie muttered, 'Oh great, that's all I need for him to stick his nose in.'

The meeting finished an hour later and the office cleared. MacKenzie read through the policy document he had written. He wanted to make sure he hadn't missed any line of enquiry.

'No,' he thought, 'that seems fine to me.'

The next few hours appeared to fly by and as 5 o'clock approached the interviewing team entered his office to give an update as to what the drug dealers were saying. It appeared as if the drug dealers were in as much of a daze over the morning's events as the police were.

MacKenzie left the office at 6 p.m. and made his way home, showered and dressed. He looked at his watch and found himself to be standing at the glossy painted black door of a block of Georgian apartments. He knocked on the door with the highly polished brass knocker. A thunderous bang rang out as the cold brass came into contact with the wood.

She answered the door and enquired if they were going straight out. MacKenzie nodded and said, 'Yes, I'm ready if you are?'

They drove off in his metallic blue coloured Ford Cougar and twenty minutes later MacKenzie pulled into the car park of the Mecca bowling alley. He parked next to a sparkling clean silver Jaguar. As he stopped he looked at the vehicle and thought to himself, 'I wish I could afford one of those.' By this time it was 7 p.m.

They both entered the bowling alley and paid ten pounds for the pleasure of having one game of ten pins. MacKenzie was handed a pair of size nine and a half shoes. He put them on and said, 'Shall I go and get some drinks, darling?'

She replied, 'Oh yes please.'

When he returned and found his girlfriend talking to another man, a slight feeling of jealously suddenly entered his head. As he approached them the man walked away.

MacKenzie said to her, 'I didn't know that you knew Paul Lomax?'

She looked at Alan and replied, 'Yes. I didn't know you knew him.'

Alan replied, 'I don't, except that he's the Home Secretary.'

After his conversation about Lomax Alan thought to himself that he hadn't discussed what exactly she did for a living except that she was a personal secretary for some bigwig. He did however think that she must have done well for herself because her apartment was in quite an expensive area.

They both enjoyed the game and they laughed at each other as one bowl after another became a comedy of errors. When they had finished the game Alan took the huff. She had won, he had been beaten on the last bowl and she had taken great pleasure in taking the Mickey out of him.

She said to Alan, 'Never mind darling I'll make it up to you.'

Alan grunted and then muttered a reply; 'Shall we go for something to eat?'

She laughed again as Alan ignored her gesture of making things up. They left the bowling alley in search for somewhere to eat.

* * *

Paul Lomax, his wife and children left the bowling alley at around 9 p.m. As he was about to leave his mobile telephone began to ring. He was hesitant to answer it. Lorraine said to him, 'Are you going to answer that or not?'

He pressed the answer button and spoke, 'Lomax.'

The voice on the other side replied, 'Parker here, the next part to the operation will commence tomorrow, are there any further instructions?'

Lomax again hesitated before his reply, almost blurting out to Parker to stop the operation, when suddenly Lorraine said, 'Who's that?'

Paul quickly replied, 'No, go ahead.' The phone went dead.

The Lomax family returned home and Lorraine couldn't help noticing the change in Paul's attitude. He seemed distant for the rest of the evening. The children thanked Paul for a good time and asked if they could go again. Lorraine was annoyed with him when he failed to reply to their request.

Lorraine thought to herself that it was since the telephone

call that his attitude changed and she attempted to find out what the problem was. It was just like talking to a brick wall. All Paul would say was, 'It'll be all right.'

Lorraine went off to bed leaving Paul in the lounge holding on to a bottle of scotch.

* * *

MacKenzie returned to his girlfriend's apartment around midnight, and seemed to find the courage to ask her if he could stay the night. He was slightly taken back when she replied to the suggestion by saying, 'Umm I don't know. Mr Policeman wants to take advantage of a poor defenceless woman does he?'

Alan smiled and as he did so, she replied, 'Why not?'

They both entered the living room and she poured them both what appeared to Alan to be a quadruple brandy. They drank and chatted until the small hours of the morning when she stood up in front of Alan and began to unbutton her silky blue blouse. She gazed into his eyes and at the same time slipped her blouse over her shoulders and let it fall to the floor. She then reached behind her back and unclipped her bra and threw it onto the armchair nearby, revealing a pair of beautiful curved breasts, her nipples erect and inviting.

Alan was almost lost in his thoughts. He couldn't believe that this beautiful woman was about to give herself to him. She took his hand and gently pulled him up from the settee. Standing in front of him she began undoing his shirt buttons. One by one she released the tension of the shirt until the last one was unfastened. She placed her arms around his body pulling him closer to her, their bodies touched and he could feel the warmth of her breasts against his chest. She gently rubbed her fingers from the bottom of Alan's back to the top; he shuddered as the feeling of intense pleasure reached his brain.

Alan gently kissed her lips and caressed her back with his hands; she smoothly turned round to allow him to kiss her neck and shoulders whilst at the same time he cupped her breasts in his hands.

She began to move her head gently from side to side; Alan's hands began to move from her breasts down across her stomach, which seemed to tense up as he continued downwards.

On reaching the top of her trousers he uncoupled the fastening and gently lowered himself to his knees, gently caressing her back as he did so. He began to pull her clothing down revealing a small pair of blue silk panties, which he also began to pull down. He caressed her bottom as she slowly turned round to reveal herself fully to him.

Alan gently led her backwards and pushed her slowly onto the settee. He kissed her body and led his tongue across her stomach, her body tensing on each stroke of his tongue. Alan removing his remaining clothing, he slipped into a passionate embrace.

She whispered in his ear, 'Please, I'm ready.'

Without hesitation Alan entered her, she gasped and a cry of wanton pleasure rang out. They made love time and time again eventually falling asleep in each other's arms.

Alan was woken by the sound of the postman pushing letters through the letterbox. He looked at his watch and muttered the word, 'Shit'. This startled her as she woke saying, 'What's the matter?'

Alan said, 'Do you know what time it is?'

She replied, 'No, what?'

He said, 'It's five to nine.'

She said, 'You're joking', as she looked at the bedside clock. 'Oh my god,' she said, 'I'm going to be late.'

'You are?' he exclaimed, 'what about me?'

Alan began to get dressed and she laughed as he fell over, trying to put his sock on standing up. She got up and went into the bathroom where she turned the shower on. 'What time do you have to be in?' she shouted.

Alan replied, 'Ten minutes ago.'

Alan picked the telephone up and rang the office; Butcher picked up the phone at the Station and heard, 'Yeah, it's MacKenzie. I'm going to be a little late in this morning.'

Butcher replied, 'OK boss, shall I delay the briefing?'

Alan replied, 'Yes. We'll have one later, then I can update the team as to what the Commissioner had to say. '

Butcher again replied, 'OK boss', and put the phone down. He thought to himself, bloody hell; he is human after all.

In all the time Butcher had known MacKenzie, he had never known MacKenzie be late for anything.

Alan looked up to see the beautiful woman who he had just spent one of the best nights of his life with, standing in front of him wrapped in a pink coloured towel.

'Do you want me to make you a drink darling?'

Alan replied, 'Yes please, I'm late anyway, it won't matter for another ten minutes or so.'

Alan enquired as to what time she was required to be in at work that morning and she informed him that fortunately she didn't have to be in until eleven. They both sat chatting over a cup of fresh morning tea and agreed to see each other later.

At 9.30 a.m. Alan closed the door of the apartment, climbed into his car and drove to the office. He thought to himself it was going to be one of those days as the journey into work appeared to take for ever as he got snarled up in the London morning traffic. He arrived in the office at just after 10 a.m.

CHAPTER FIVE

Alan Duncan MacKenzie entered his office. It was the first time he had been late for work in fifteen years. Butcher entered his office carrying a mug of tea and updated Alan on any recent findings.

Alan asked, 'What about the interviews?'

Butcher replied 'There's nothing Sir. It would appear that the dealers know nothing about this other gang.'

'Right, ' he said, 'I'm off home to get changed, then I'm going to see the Commissioner.'

'Did you have a good night Sir?' Butcher cheekily asked.

'Why?' Alan enquired.

'I just thought that you didn't get home last night.' Butcher paused. 'Well ... '

Alan ignored the question and left saying, 'You know where I am if you need me.'

Alan returned home and quickly changed into a clean shirt and put his best suit on. Within minutes he was off to see the Commissioner.

As he pulled into the car park, Alan found that the entrance was blocked by a mass of press and photographers. He had to push his way to the entrance and was greeted in the foyer by the concierge who said, 'Can I help you, Sir?'

Alan stated that he had an appointment with the Commissioner at 11 a.m. The concierge handed Alan a nametag, which he stuck to his jacket pocket, and said, 'If you take the lift to the third floor, turn right and go through the swing doors, you will find his secretary there.'

Alan acknowledged the instructions given to him and crossed the foyer to the lift and pressed the button requesting the lift to descend.

After a few seconds the lift came to a stop on the ground floor, the doors opened and people started to walk out. Alan entered the lift, pressed the third floor button, the doors closed and the lift commenced to ascend.

Alan looked into the wall mirror in the lift and rubbed his chin. He thought to himself, you could have done with a shave before you came out, god you look rough.

The lift came to an abrupt stop, the doors opened and Alan got out, he walked through the right hand swing doors which said 'No Entry, Official Personnel Only.'

Once inside a middle-aged female said, 'Can I help you?'

MacKenzie introduced himself stating that he had an appointment with the Commissioner at 11 a.m.

'Oh yes Sir,' she replied, 'he's expecting you but he's running a little behind schedule. If you take a seat in the waiting room I'll call you as soon as he is free.'

Alan took a seat in the waiting room when another younger female entered and asked if he would like a cup of coffee. He said, 'Yes please.'

The young female returned a few minutes later carrying a tray which held a cafetiére of coffee, cup and saucer and half a dozen biscuits on a plate. Alan thought to himself that this was a bit of all right and that he'd have to get Butcher better trained! Twenty minutes later he was summoned into the Commissioner's office, where he received a warm greeting from the Commissioner.

Alan saw that the Commissioner was in company with a female and three other males. The Commissioner introduced them as being two top ranking officials from Customs and

Excise, his Staff Officer and the female as his Press Officer.

As he entered, Alan wished that he had now visited the toilet instead of having that second cup of coffee, which seemed to have gone right through him.

Sir Michael Collins had been the Commissioner for the past eighteen months, and he invited Alan to take a seat. The Commissioner commenced the meeting by saying that he had read the interim report which Alan had submitted surrounding the incident involving the consignment of drugs. He then asked Alan for a progress report.

Alan said, 'Well Sir, the enquiry is still in its infancy.' Alan paused and thought to himself that the word infancy was a little posh for him and continued by saying, 'There is no progress at present, the interviews with the drug dealers have not produced any fresh evidence. At the moment we are at a loss as to who were involved.' Alan assured the meeting that all usual lines of enquiry were being sought, but to date had proved negative.

A general discussion took place and the meeting ended with the Commissioner thanking everyone for coming and stating that he had a press conference to attend. As Alan was about to leave, the Commissioner called him over and quietly whispered in his ear, 'I need your help on this one Alan, there's a lot of people out there watching this case. Do your best.'

Alan replied, 'I will, Sir.'

'Good luck,' was the Commissioner's reply as Alan left the room.

Alan's exit from the building was easier than when he came as the press had gone into the press hall. The car park was clear as he climbed into his car and drove away.

Once back in his office Alan again reviewed his policy document. He was struggling to think of any ideas, he did however, find that he had duplicated himself on two occasions.

At 4 p.m. Alan headed a briefing, nothing fresh had come

from the gathering. He was informed that the eight drug dealers had been charged and would be appearing at the Magistrates' Court in the morning.

Alan asked the Custom and Excise Officers if any of their sources had furnished anything. 'No,' was the reply.

The following Sunday night Alan visited his girlfriend, again staying the night. He did however, make a vow that he wouldn't be late to work again, he was of the opinion that nothing seemed to go right when you're late in.

At 6.30 a.m. Monday morning Alan's mobile phone rang. He woke to the sound of a female's voice whispering in his ear, 'Alan wake up, it's your phone.'

Alan still waking up said, 'What? Yeah.'

He picked the phone up and said, 'MacKenzie.'

'Good morning boss,' was the reply, 'I tried to get you at home.' It was Frank Butcher.

'What do you want?' Alan said, as he sat up in bed.

Alan's attention was stopped slightly as he watched the shapely figure of a female form getting out of bed. 'What do you want Frank?' he repeated.

Butcher appeared excited and said, 'There has been a development, the diving section were doing a training exercise yesterday at Victoria Dock. It would appear as if they have located our vehicles.'

Alan asked, 'Have you arranged for their recovery?'

'Yes, it's happening as we talk,' was the reply.

Alan told Butcher that he would meet him at the dock.

As the telephone went dead Alan saw this beautiful vision return. He said, 'You should be careful, you'll catch your death of cold.' She handed him a fresh cup of tea, which he placed onto the bedside cabinet next to him.

'Come here,' he said as he pulled her towards him. Their bodies met.

'I thought you had to go?' she said.

'It can wait,' he replied as he put his arms around her, twisted her over onto her back and rolled on top of her. She chuckled and shuddered at the same time as Alan moved his fingers up and down her spine. They made love.

Half an hour later Alan got out of bed, dressed and kissed her goodbye. On leaving he shouted, 'I'll ring you.'

Alan turned up at Victoria Dock where he saw that the recovery was well under way. He saw that two of the armoured jeeps were already standing on the dock dripping water from underneath. He looked across the dock and could see two police divers in the water; one of the divers had his thumb up, which was indicating to the crane driver that he could commence to lift the next vehicle. The crane moved into action and Alan could see the tension of the lifting wire becoming taut, he could smell a strong odour of diesel in the air as the crane's engine revved louder and louder.

Butcher noticed Alan standing at the dockside and approached him saying, 'At least we can start on some proper enquiries now Sir.'

Slowly, inch by inch, the vehicle began emerging from its watery grave. As it cleared the water, the sound of water pouring out of the vehicle was like that of a waterfall cascading into a lake below.

The crane lifted the vehicle over the water to the dockside where it was gently lowered to the ground. Alan informed Frank Butcher that he wanted an immediate examination of the vehicles.

Frank replied, 'The Scenes of Crime are just turning up now, Sir.'

Alan said, 'Can you put one of the enquiry teams on to the vehicle side straight away?'

The following morning's briefing revealed that the initial

examination of the vehicles other than the Volvo tractor unit had produced nothing of any significant evidential value. The Scenes of Crime Officer stated that the person or persons disposing of the vehicles had gone to some lengths to remove all forms of identification marks including the engine number.

The officer summed up by saying, 'However I'm hoping that a Spectron Microscope examination might reveal something. It will take about a week before we know.'

Alan MacKenzie asked, 'Do we know anything at all about them?'

The Scenes Officer continued, saying, 'All the jeeps were fitted with automatic machine guns, these too had all their identifying marks removed. They have already been sent to the laboratory for further examination. They are of a type which is commonly used by mercenaries.'

Alan repeated, 'Mercenaries.'

'Yes,' came back the reply.

Alan paused and thought to himself that this was not a line of enquiry he had considered. He made a note of it in his briefing book.

Alan then looked at Inspector Bob Thompson, who had been put in charge of the vehicle enquiry team and said, 'I want your team to get round all the suppliers of these vehicles, Bob and I'll put another team to look at the firearms side of things.'

Bob Thompson nodded in reply. The Scenes of Crime Officer then finished off by informing the briefing that all the vehicles had been wiped clean before being dumped in the dock, except for the articulated tractor unit. In this case no effort had been made to erase any of its identifying marks, however there wouldn't have been a need to do so as the vehicle's history was already known to the Customs enquiry. He concluded, 'We did recover a balaclava helmet, which was army issue. There is a possibility of obtaining DNA as there are hairs on this item, again it will take a couple of weeks to get the examination done. We're having to rely on the lab to fit us in.'

Alan shouted across the room probably a little more loudly than he intended, 'Get it done, fast track it! It doesn't matter at this stage if it costs more, we need it.'

The Scenes Officer went red in the face, thinking that Alan was having a go at him by the tone of his voice. He replied, 'Yes, Sir.'

The briefing ended and Alan returned to his room. 'You were a bit hard on the SOCO officer Sir, if you don't mind me saying?' Butcher said.

Alan paused for a while and replied, 'Yes you're right Frank, I'll speak to him.'

MacKenzie immediately picked the telephone up and spoke to the SOCO officer and apologised for his manner earlier.

* * *

The mobile telephone rang, Paul Lomax hesitated before he answered it, he knew that Parker would be on the other end.

He answered it, 'Yes.'

Parker replied, 'All transactions have now been completed, you shall see the results very soon.'

Lomax ended the call by saying, 'Yes OK, thank you for a very well executed operation, I suggest that our contract could now be terminated.'

The phone went dead.

Lomax sat for a while in his office gazing into space, before he realised half an hour had gone by when he was abruptly interrupted. Helen walked into the office and placed another pile of paperwork into Paul's in tray.

* * *

Parker was standing in the kitchen at the farmhouse. He opened the top grate of the kitchen stove and carefully began to remove papers he had gathered in the buff folder, which had the words 'for your eyes only' on it. One by one he placed the papers into the fire below. Parker stood with a smile on his face as he watched the flames rise out of the stove.

He placed the last page from the folder into the fire then crumpled the folder up and placed it too into the fire. He then picked up a poker and began stabbing at the embers ensuring that all the documents, maps and plans had been destroyed.

Parker then shouted for Evans, who entered the kitchen saying, 'Yes Sir'.

Parker requested Evans to tell all the men to regroup in the barn in two weeks' time, Tuesday night at 22.00 hours.

'Yes Sir,' Evans again replied.

* * *

By mid afternoon of that day MacKenzie was hoping to get away early, but his plans were upset when the Uniform Inspector knocked on his office door and walked in.

'Have you got five minutes to spare Sir?' he asked.

Alan replied, 'Yes if you're quick.'

The Inspector continued, 'We have had a problem today. We have been inundated with suspected overdoses and sudden deaths among the drug fraternity.'

Alan asked, 'How many?'

The Inspector replied, 'We've had twenty this morning and about the same in overdoses.'

'What, twenty dead?' repeated Alan.

The reply was, 'Yes.'

Alan asked, 'Are any of these deaths linked in any way?'

The Inspector looked at Alan and said, 'At the present time we are unable to say. However I understand that deaths are occurring all over the city.'

Alan requested that he should be kept updated as the events unfolded. A discussion took place between them to argue the fact that the CID should get involved at this early stage. The Inspector left the office feeling a bit bemused.

Alan appeared to be less concerned about what he had just been told, dismissing the problem. He thought about the job in hand, wondering if Butcher had anything to do for the morning briefing. On satisfying himself that he had nothing to do, Alan left the office saying that he was going to see someone.

CHAPTER SIX

At 10 a.m. the following morning Mark Carter, the Junior Minister for Health was sitting in his office. He had spent the last hour answering the telephone. As soon as he got to work the telephone rang and as soon as he put the phone down it rang again.

A number of hospitals around the City had become alarmed over the number of deaths which had occurred over the last twenty-four hours. In the City alone over one thousand had been recorded and the figure was rising. What was even more alarming to him was that he had just received a telephone call from one of the local health authorities outside the City who was experiencing similar problems.

Mark Carter left his office and crossed the corridor and entered another office. He spoke to the secretary sat at the desk. 'Sam, is she in?' Mark asked.

She replied, 'Yes, she's just walked in.'

Without further ado Mark walked straight into the adjoining office and confronted the Secretary for Health, the Right Honourable Joanna Brown MP.

'What's the matter Mark?' she asked.

Carter informed her of what had been happening around the City and suggested to her that similar occurrences had begun to happen around the country.

'How bad is it?' she asked.

'It's well over a thousand now,' he replied.

She suggested that Mark should personally monitor the

situation and keep her updated over any developments. As the day went by nearly every health authority in the country had contacted the Ministry. Deaths were occurring in their hundreds all over.

Maxwell was in his office when the telephone rang. He answered it. 'Hello Joanna, how are you?'

Maxwell went silent as Joanna informed him as to what had been happening. He asked, 'How many?'

She replied, 'Thousands, but we do not have an exact figure as yet.'

'I'll come to your office straight away,' he said and put the phone down immediately.

Maxwell left his office and as he did so told his secretary to summon his car. He left Number 10 and was at the Ministry of Health in ten minutes. He was escorted to Joanna's office. He entered and demanded to be updated as to the latest death rate.

'At the moment the figure is just reaching seven thousand across the Metropolitan District, and that is not counting the number of suspected overdoses taken to hospital.' After taking her breath she said, 'That figure is rising very quickly.'

Maxwell said, 'Do we know the cause as yet?'

'No not as yet, it is too early to say what the cause is,' she replied.

Maxwell asked what she was doing regarding the matter to which she informed him that she had set up an incident room to record all data and had requested to be informed of what the actual cause of deaths were in each case.

Maxwell left the Ministry of Health not a happy man, he thought to himself that was all he needed on top of his crime problems. He decided at this stage not to hold a press conference. On returning to his office he requested his secretary to get hold of Lomax and get him to the office as soon as possible. After an hour Lomax entered Number 10 and asked,

'What's the panic about?'

He was shown to the Prime Minister's office. There he saw a very worried man sat in an armchair near to the fireplace. 'What the hell's the matter?' Lomax asked.

Maxwell began to tell him what was happening. Lomax did not seem surprised.

* * *

MacKenzie had just finished the morning briefing when he was summoned to the Commissioner's office. 'Not again,' he muttered to himself. 'This is getting to be a habit.'

MacKenzie knew that something was on because this time there was a uniform marked car waiting to take him to the Commissioner's office. Alan climbed into the vehicle and as soon as he had fastened his seat belt the driver switched on the blue flashing lights and siren of the police car. They dashed through the busy traffic and arrived at the Commissioner's office within minutes.

MacKenzie got out of the vehicle and was greeted at the door by the concierge who on this occasion didn't bother giving him a name tag or pass the time of day, but escorted him personally straight to the Commissioner's office.

On entering the office MacKenzie saw that Sir Michael Collins was already in company with the people who he had met on the previous occasion. The Commissioner, on this occasion did not greet Alan MacKenzie but immediately said to all in the room, 'I have brought you all here because a problem has arisen all over the country which may have some bearing on current investigations.' He continued by informing the gathering of what had happened in the last twenty-four hours.

MacKenzie was the first to speak after the Commissioner had concluded what he was saying. As he was about to speak the office door opened and the Commissioner's secretary brought in a trolley which had cups, saucers and tea and coffee. 'Thank you' the Commissioner said as she left.

Alan then remarked, 'Why do we think that these deaths are linked to my enquiry?'

The Commissioner explained, 'Early indications are that the drug involved is heroin, and that it is of a similar source to that which Customs had under surveillance, which was stolen. This has still to be confirmed, although initial findings have shown this. But I thought that your early involvement would be the right course of action at this time.'

'Oh my god' MacKenzie said. 'This puts my investigation into a different ball game altogether.'

The Commissioner agreed, then stated that at the present there was a press blackout, although he didn't think that the press would take long to pick the problem up.

The Commissioner concluded by saying that all of them were to be at Number 10 Downing Street for a meeting with the Prime Minister at 3 p.m. His last words were 'Don't be late'.

Each of the persons at the meeting returned to their respective offices to collate any up-to-date intelligence on their enquiries. Alan informed Butcher of what had occurred and told him to get the team together, ready for when he returned from the Prime Minister's office. On leaving the office he instructed Frank, 'Nothing is to be said outside this office. Do you understand Frank, nothing. I don't want any leaks from our end, otherwise the shit will really hit the fan.'

At 3 p.m. exactly on time a meeting was convened at Number 10 Downing Street. Alan couldn't believe that he had been elevated to such a position that he was sat around a table with some of the top people in the country.

At the meeting were Maxwell and Paul Lomax, whom he recalled seeing talking to his girlfriend at the Mecca bowling alley. Joanna Brown was also present, and the Commissioner was there as well. Alan took a seat next to him. The meeting lasted an hour and in Alan's eyes it was a total waste of time. He was on his own with his thoughts as everyone else thought that the meeting was productive.

A heated discussion took place over the subject of the press. Lomax had persuaded Maxwell not to hold a press conference until a positive link had been established with the drugs, and he informed the Prime Minister that he understood a confirmation would soon be forthcoming. He also stated that he had personally requested a speedy result in that respect. It was discovered that because of the numbers of deaths involved that it would be two to three days before the laboratory could confirm or deny any link.

What the others at the meeting didn't know was that the longer the delay the better it was for Lomax's plan. Lomax stated that he would take personal responsibility over the press.

The meeting ended with all agreeing that they should reconvene at 3 p.m. the following day. Alan was trying to think of ways in which he could miss the next meeting, but the Commissioner told him that he wished him to be present at the meeting. It was said in a tone that MacKenzie knew to be an instruction and not a request.

Alan returned to his office at a more leisurely pace than he left. On entering his office he made a telephone call.

'Hi, it's me,' he said. 'I'm going to have to cancel tonight, something major has come up, I hope you don't mind?'

A short conversation took place as Butcher entered the office and placed a note in front of him stating that the team was ready for him. 'Sorry darling, I'll have to go.' Alan replaced the telephone down onto the receiver.

MacKenzie attended the briefing and informed his team that the enquiry had stepped up a notch or two. He outlined the events of the day. He told his team that the parameters of the enquiry would be extended to cover any terrorist groups and anti-drug campaigns. This could mean that they would have more personnel joining the team, which he believed would cause problems of management.

He concluded the briefing by telling everyone to go home except for Butcher and the enquiry team Inspectors, saying that there would be a few late nights ahead.

* * *

Lomax returned to his office and asked Helen if she could stay later that night. She replied that she had to rearrange her evening but didn't think that his request would pose her a problem, She already knew that her evening had been cancelled but thought she would impress Lomax by saying she would rearrange her commitment. He thanked her for her co-operation and then informed her of the day's events. As he looked at Helen he found it strange that she didn't appear to be surprised by what he had told her, he dismissed this by saying to himself that she knew everything normally anyway.

Helen commenced at Lomax's dictation a number of letters that he wanted delivering by hand before she left that night. She did not understand why it was so important for these letters to go that night, as they did not seem to her to be important. She felt however that something was playing on Paul's mind. On the conclusion of him dictating he said to Helen, 'Things are going to change round here over the next few months and you are going to be part of that, Helen.'

Helen smiled and said, 'I know.'

Lomax looked at her curiously and wondered what she meant by that reply, his mind was buzzing and he gave her remark little more attention. He thanked her again for staying at work as she went off to type her letters.

* * *

MacKenzie spent most of the night sitting in conference with his Inspectors, examining lines of enquiry and arguing over which enquiry should take priority. He left the office exhausted at 3 a.m.

He was still thinking when he got home. He poured himself a glass of scotch, sat down in his armchair with a note-pad and began scribbling away. He was under no illusions now as to the seriousness of his investigation. He was also aware of the attention he and his team were going to get. He knew everything had to be done right. If any member of his team failed, he failed.

Alan woke to find himself still in the armchair, he couldn't recall going to sleep but wished he hadn't because his neck was stiff and painful. He showered, dressed and was back in the office by 7.30 a.m.

Frank Butcher arrived at the office at quarter to eight and was amazed to find MacKenzie sat at his desk. 'Good morning, Sir,' he shouted through the office door, returning fifteen minutes later with a hot mug of tea and a paper bag containing a bacon and mushroom sandwich. 'Thought you might need this Sir,' he said as he grinned and passed the white paper bag over to him. Alan replied with a stern, 'Thank you.'

Before the morning briefing Alan received a telephone call from Joanna Brown who gave him even more alarming news of overnight developments. The deaths had risen to just over thirty-five thousand. Alan sat back in his chair stunned and speechless.

'Alan are you there?' Joanna shouted down the phone.

'I'm sorry,' he said. 'Did I hear you right?'

Joanna replied 'Yes,' and continued, saying that the rate of deaths had now started to reduce. The Prime Minister had called for an earlier meeting; it had been rearranged for 11 a.m. Before Alan put the telephone down he informed Joanna that he would be at the meeting. He was stunned by the news he had heard and entered the morning briefing more determined than ever to get the person responsible for committing such a crime.

The room was full of seasoned detectives who were whispering among themselves. As Alan informed them of how many people had died the room became silent; you could hear a pin drop. Nobody could believe what he had said.

The briefing produced nothing new in the investigation. Alan concluded it by saying that the team would be pulling out all the stops on this enquiry, no stone would remain unturned. 'We have to be thorough and come up with a result quickly on this one,' he said.

As soon as Alan left the briefing room the audience boomed with chatter, the death rate involved was unbelievable. None of those present in that room had been involved in such a high profile enquiry. From out of the mêlée someone was heard saying loudly 'This is the sort of thing that happens in America, not here. What the hell's going on?' This summed it up for the whole team and they too left the briefing with a sense of urgency.

Alan attended the 11 o'clock meeting at Number 10. The press had already got hold of the news and as Alan arrived outside Number 10 he saw that the area was inundated with correspondents from around the world. The nearby roads were all congested with every kind of television broadcast vehicle with satellite dishes of every conceivable shape and size.

Alan passed by the clicking of cameras and was given immediate access to the building. The meeting commenced dead on eleven o'clock. Alan sat down round a large highly polished mahogany table; the walls were painted white, and hung around at regulated spaces were paintings of previous Prime Ministers.

Maxwell headed the meeting, the number of people attending it had doubled, and all sat quiet with stern-looking faces. Alan looked at Joanna Brown who smiled and nodded to him. Alan returned the gesture with a firm nod.

Maxwell started the meeting by confirming the death rate figures given by Joanna and stated that he would be holding a press conference straight after the meeting. When Maxwell had finished an elderly man aged about sixty stood up and addressed the room. He introduced himself as Professor Armstrong, the head of the Home Office Forensic Science Laboratory.

The Professor stated that ninety-five per cent of the deaths had occurred from a combination of heroin and strychnine poison, which together had caused a painful but certain death.

He continued his presentation by saying that the examination of blood samples taken from the deceased had revealed that the heroin consumed into the body, was, with a ninety-nine per cent certainty, the same as that which was stolen a few weeks ago from the consignment being observed by the Custom and Excise. This was known because prior to the shipment being stolen the Customs enquiry team had obtained a sample in order to confirm it was a controlled drug.

MacKenzie paused and thought that they had got the result of confirmation back from the lab quickly. He chuckled to himself thinking that if he had requested the lab to hurry up with a result, he'd still be waiting.

Maxwell thanked Armstrong for his presentation and said, 'As you can see ladies and gentlemen, at some point a person or persons have contaminated the drugs with this poison. This is a case of mass murder.'

Maxwell continued by appointing the Chief Constable of the Devon and Cornwall Police, Sir Peter Ashbourne to oversee the enquiry. However Chief Inspector MacKenzie would continue to lead the investigation. Maxwell asked if anyone else in the room wished to add anything then stated he was going to do the press conference.

Paul Lomax sat throughout the entire meeting doodling on his note pad, at one point his eyebrows raised when Maxwell stated that against his better judgement, he was advised not to go to the press before. Maxwell felt that maybe by doing so he could have prevented some of the deaths occurring by warning the public of the dangers of taking the drug.

MacKenzie interrupted Maxwell to ask, 'Are you going to make reference to the link between the deaths and the stolen drugs?'

Maxwell replied, 'Yes,' and stated that he didn't have any option, as the press would link it anyway. He ended by saying, 'This is a murder investigation and they will be told so.'

As people began to leave the meeting MacKenzie stood up and thought to himself that at least he wouldn't have to attend all these meetings, now that the Chief Constable had been appointed to head the enquiry. That meant he could get on with the job of investigating.

Later that afternoon the Prime Minister appeared on national television and was met with a barrage of questions from the media. Maxwell got what he anticipated, the questions were tough but he managed to brush them aside as easily as if answering questions across the floor of the House.

CHAPTER SEVEN

The days went by and the enquiry entered its second week as a murder investigation. Alan hadn't seen much of his new girlfriend because he appeared to be working 'all hours god sends'. They had however kept in touch over the telephone. She too had been working longer hours recently.

There had been a slight breakthrough in the enquiry; the forensic laboratory had finally completed their examinations of the recovered vehicles used in the raid at the breaker's yard.

The morning's briefing began with a summary of the findings. The Scenes of Crimes Officer began by saying that as everybody was aware, the engine numbers on all the vehicles, apart from the tractor unit had been eradicated. The Spectron Microscope examination did however produce engine numbers on two out of the four vehicles. Likewise with the serial numbers on the weapons, they had also produced results.

The officer continued, 'In respect of the balaclava found, DNA has been found on the hair specimen and this is at present being checked against all known data bases.'

Inspector Thompson, who was leading the team enquiring into the vehicles, stood up. He informed the gathering that his team's enquiries revealed that the two army vehicles had in fact come from the Catterick Army barracks. 'We will be going up there later today, to find the ins and out of their disappearance. It appears that someone managed to walk away with four such vehicles and we are liaising with the Military Police in this respect.'

He continued by saying that the firearms had come from a difference source, which he would first discuss with Mr MacKenzie about how they would approach the army on this matter.

Alan butted in, saying, 'I need your team to get up to Catterick after this briefing. I need to know how and when those vehicles went, and I desperately need a name or description of who picked them up.'

Inspector Thompson replied, 'Yes Sir, we'll get onto it right away.'

Alan then requested an update as to how the poison enquiry was getting on. The reply back was 'Not very well Sir.'

Alan said, 'Somebody must be missing it, and the quantity we're talking about is just mind-blowing.'

Butcher stated, 'That's the problem boss, no one wants to admit to such a large amount going missing.'

Alan replied, 'OK, but stick at it, once it's been identified I think we'll obtain some good information from there.'

'Very well everybody. At last we have some definite lines of enquiry. I'll see you tomorrow,' Alan said as he concluded the briefing.

The briefing ended and Alan returned to his office. He picked the telephone up and pressed the digits. The phone was answered after two rings. 'Hi it's me,' Alan said.

'Hello darling, long time no hear,' she replied.

Alan said, 'I know but it's been bedlam here, can we get together, tonight maybe?'

A smile came on Alan's face as she replied, 'I would love to.'

He said, 'I'll see you about eight at your place,' and replaced the phone.

Inspector Thompson entered MacKenzie's office. He closed the door and stated that he wished to speak about the firearms recovered from the dock. 'Yes what's the problem?' Alan enquired.

Thompson explained that it had been confirmed that the weapons were in fact army issue, however when they tried to get any details from the army, they were being blanked. Apparently that information was top secret.

Alan instructed Thompson to push the issue when he got up to Catterick but stated, 'If there is still a problem get back to me before you leave.'

Inspector Thompson and his team made a slow journey up the A1 to Catterick camp, arriving there around 4 p.m. A pompous Sergeant Major Lewis of the Military Police met him and his team. Thompson and the rest of the team were shown to overnight accommodation on the camp. Thompson tried to arrange a meeting with Sergeant Major Lewis that evening but the Sergeant Major sternly stated that he was off duty at 5 p.m. and would be unable to see him until 10 a.m. the next day.

On leaving, the Sergeant Major remarked to Thompson, 'If you think you 'civvi police' can come here and start telling us what to do, you're wrong.' He then left.

Alan was still in his office when he gazed at his watch, 7 p.m. 'Oh god,' he thought to himself. He dashed out of the office and told Butcher if he was wanted he would be on his mobile.

Before Butcher could reply he had gone. 'I was going home myself anyway,' he thought.

It was a typical journey home, Alan thought. When you want to get moving you catch every red traffic light, and traffic just seems to crawl along. He arrived home, showered and dressed and arrived at his girlfriend's front door half an hour late.

She answered the door and said with a smile, 'Tut tut. Fancy keeping a girl waiting.'

'I know, I know,' he replied, 'but the hours just fly by at the moment and the traffic was terrible.'

They spent the evening in, passing the time away on what

had been happening in each other's life over the past few days. She asked Alan if he wanted to stay the night. He declined the offer saying that he had to be up early the next morning. As he grabbed his jacket to leave she said, 'You're not going off me already, are you?'

Alan replied, 'Don't be silly, you're the best thing that's happened to me for a long time.'

As the door closed behind him he stopped on the pavement and wondered if he was letting the job get in the way of his private life again. He was determined not to let that happen again.

The following day MacKenzie arrived at the office before Butcher arrived and began reading through the mountain of statements already generated from the enquiry. At 9.30 a.m. he had a meeting with the Chief bringing him up to speed about the forensic side of the enquiry and what enquiries were on going at that time.

Before leaving the Chief's office, Alan suggested that maybe the other force areas should be arresting the drug dealers to see if they could get any further information from that side. The Chief replied that it could produce a lot more work for the team but agreed that it was a line of enquiry which should be followed.

'If only to remove any unused drugs,' Alan explained.

'I'll get on to it today,' the Chief said.

Inspector Thompson met with Sergeant Major Lewis as arranged at 10 a.m. The meeting started badly with Lewis informing Thompson that the Military Police were not happy with the civilian Police conducting enquiries on the camp.

It was obvious to Thompson that Lewis was being obstructive from the start.

Thompson listed things to Lewis that he required to know. They included all the information about the army vehicles that went missing and the circumstances surrounding their disappearance. Thompson stated that he required any paper work regarding the vehicles and especially acquisition papers which allowed persons to remove the vehicles. Thompson said, 'I need to speak to all the personnel who had anything to do with the people who picked the vehicles up.'

Sergeant Major Lewis looked at Thompson and gave him a surly grin, and informed him that a lot of the information which had been requested was classified and he would be unable to provide it. In addition he stated that Thompson would be unable to interview any of the army personnel.

Thompson said to Lewis, 'Do you realise the importance of what I am requesting from you?'

Lewis replied, 'I couldn't give a damn, we shall do any enquiries on this camp.'

Thompson asked, 'By "we", do you mean you?'

Lewis replied, 'You're on my camp and I'll say who does what.'

Thompson asked if he could make a telephone call, which he did.

'Good morning Sir, it's Thompson here, I am having problems at this end.' He began telling the story of Lewis's attitude and of what had been happening in the camp. Alan said, 'I'll get back to you.' He placed his finger down on the receiver button and began pressing the numbers on the phone. The phone was answered and Alan related the story to the person on the other end.

Following the telephone call MacKenzie telephoned Catterick camp and again spoke to Thompson. 'The problem has been sorted,' he said. At that very moment the door to the office opened, Sergeant Major Lewis stood to attention and the Camp Commandant entered the room. 'I think it's just happened,' Thompson replied. 'I'll get back to you later.' Thompson replaced the telephone onto the receiver.

The Commandant said to Thompson, 'I understand you have been having a few problems with co-operation Inspector?'

'A little, Sir,' replied Thompson.

'Sergeant Major Lewis you are relieved. I shall be assisting the Inspector from now on. I'll see you in my office shortly,' the Commandant announced in a stern and authoritative manner.

'Yes Sir,' the Sergeant Major shouted, he then saluted and before leaving the office gave Thompson a look which could kill. It was obvious to Thompson that Lewis had had his nose put out of place.

'Now then, how can I help, Inspector?' the Commandant asked.

Thompson repeated his requests.

Within the hour Sergeant Major Lewis returned to the office where Thompson and the Camp Commandant were collating their enquiries, and handed to the Commandant a bundle of papers.

The papers were handed to Thompson who found that the army records were very comprehensive and gave every possible detail relating to each of the two vehicles identified from the engine numbers. In addition the Commandant stated that three days after the two vehicles were picked up the same two army personnel collected a further two vehicles, and gave him the files in relation to those vehicles.

Thompson replied, 'That's excellent, thank you very much,' as he took hold of the files.

Thompson turned to the Commandant and said, 'Without treading on anyone's toes, Sir. Just how easy is it for someone to forge these documents and to enter the camp and collect these vehicles?'

The Commandant paused and said, 'I would like to say that

it was impossible for someone to do that, from outside. I feel that this could only be done by either army personnel or someone with army experience.'

'So are we saying that it's impossible for an outsider or not?' he repeated.

The Commandant sighed and said, 'Well, as you may realise from your experience Inspector, nothing is impossible, but it is very unlikely.'

'Can I thank you for your frankness, Commandant,' the Inspector said gratefully. 'I would however like to speak to anyone who may have had dealings with the people who picked the vehicles up.'

The Commandant stated that it wouldn't be a problem and assured that the Army would co-operate fully in this investigation. The rest of Thompson's day was spent interviewing army personnel. Before ending the day he made a telephone call to MacKenzie to update him on the day's events.

MacKenzie, prior to putting the telephone down, asked how long Thompson's team would take. 'Three or four days' he replied.

'Don't forget to enquire about the weapons,' Alan prompted Thompson.

'No Sir,' he replied.

During that day Alan MacKenzie had been having meetings with high-ranking officials from the department of Customs and Excise. He had to examine the possibility of a leak of information from their department. It was decided that they would conduct any enquiries in that respect in secret.

Commander Kenneth Jones informed the meeting that the only person he had spoken to outside his department was the Home Secretary, Lomax. It was agreed that Lomax was a safe contact. MacKenzie informed those present at the meeting that research into the Customs Officers' background would have to be considered and offered the assistance of any kind to them. He ended that meeting by saying 'Yours is a thankless task which if not treated gently could disrupt your department greatly, I shall be doing the same in respect to the firearms team assigned to the initial incident.'

Three days went by, and as Alan entered the office Butcher told him that Joanna Brown had been trying to get hold of him. 'Do you know why?' he asked.

Butcher shook his head and said, 'No she didn't say but it sounded important.'

Before taking his coat off Alan telephoned Joanna, and she informed him that there had been another increase in death related incidents involving drug takers.

Alan said to her, 'I was afraid that this might happen, I think it would be because the drug dealers are trying to off-load any remaining drugs they have.' He paused and said, 'To them it's just money, they don't consider the victims.'

Alan replaced the telephone and updated Butcher; 'I'm off to see the Chief,' he said and promptly left the office. Alan knocked on the door of Chief Constable Ashbourne's office. He entered. 'Sorry Sir, but your secretary's not around.'

'Come in Alan,' he shouted across the room.

Alan informed the Chief of his earlier conversation with Joanna Brown. Following his discussion with Alan the Chief decided that more forceful action had to be taken around the country to prevent the flow of contaminated drugs. He requested his secretary to come into the office and instructed her to contact all Police Force Chief Constables so that he could speak to them personally. She left his office and immediately began her task in alphabetical order.

The Chief Constable, Sir Peter Ashbourne instructed each of the other Chief Constables of the urgency of removing drugs off the streets. He informed them that any means necessary could be used. 'We must stop these deaths,' he stated.

By the end of the day he was exhausted and fed up with hearing his voice repeating the same instructions time and time again.

Two more days had gone by and the daily briefing commenced on time. Inspector Thompson and his team had returned from Catterick and Alan quickly allowed him to give his presentation to the gathering. Half an hour had gone by when Thompson stated that one of the persons they were looking for was described as being 'a white male in his late thirties or early forties, of muscular build. He has short cut dark hair, which is greying. He has a square looking face, sporting a moustache and has very noticeable eyebrows. This man was dressed in army uniform, that of a Major.'

He paused and said, 'It was thought by all Army Personnel that this Major carried his uniform well and appeared very genuine.'

Thompson paused again to allow anyone taking notes to catch up, then continued, 'This man was accompanied by a second white male, possibly younger with a Welsh accent. We have no other details. He too was wearing army uniform.'

Thompson informed the briefing that the vehicles had been stolen about two weeks prior to the incident at the breaker's yard, two vehicles being taken on two separate occasions.

He ended his presentation by saying that the army believed that these two people were either serving members of the army or had recently left. They were of the opinion that only persons with army knowledge would know the system of collecting any army equipment and having the required paperwork.

MacKenzie asked, 'What about the weapons?'

Thompson replied, 'I'll have to speak to you about that after the briefing, but at present we have no information.'

MacKenzie then said, 'Have we considered photofits for these two?'

'Yes Sir, the witnesses are travelling down today to do that,' he replied.

Alan then looked around the briefing room and repeated the question he had asked at every briefing, 'What about the poison?'

Butcher stated that there was no change on that matter.

'DNA?' Alan grunted.

'We're still searching on that, Sir,' the Scenes of Crime Officer replied.

The briefing ended with a little more excitement, as now there was a description of a possible suspect. Alan returned to his office followed by Thompson. 'Well?' Alan said.

Thompson began by saying that he didn't know whom the boss had spoken too but the Commandant at Catterick couldn't be more helpful. 'However when we spoke about the weapons, all he could say was that the weapons belonged to the army, but he was unable to give any further information about them. It would appear that his level of authority did not allow him to divulge any information of that matter. He gave me a hint, SAS.'

Alan went silent, 'I thought so,' he said. 'It had all the hallmarks of SAS.'

With military precision the army witnesses attended at the Force Intelligence Office where the photo-fit was to be made up. MacKenzie decided to attend as well. He wanted to see the face of the person who was callous enough to poison thousands of people.

The first witness completed his description and slowly frame by frame a face appeared on screen. Alan's heart rushed for a second as the operator pressed the print button of the computer. Out of the printer came the first picture of the prime suspect in the enquiry.

At first glance Alan was quiet as he wondered, how can this man be so careless to allow himself to be recognised so easily? Are any of his facial features a disguise? Or did he think himself so clever that we wouldn't be able to trace the vehicles?

There were three witnesses who produced photo-fit pictures of the suspect and when Alan examined each photo-fit in turn he could see that all the witnesses had produced a similar description. 'This has got to be him,' he muttered to himself.

Alan handed the photo-fits to Butcher saying. 'Get these photostatted straight away, I want every member of the team to have one.'

'I'll need some spare for the Chief,' he shouted as Butcher opened the door to leave.

CHAPTER EIGHT

It was now a fortnight since Parker instructed his men to regroup on Tuesday.

The day began as usual for Alan MacKenzie, except he now had a face to his suspect. He had updated the Chief who congratulated him and his team for their efforts so far. He handed over copies of the three photo-fits to the Chief.

The Chief said, 'Thank you for these, I have a meeting this afternoon, it would be nice to give them something for a change.'

Alan left the Chief and returned to his office where he made a telephone call to his girlfriend. He arranged another night out but this time asked if she minded if he stayed the night.

She replied, 'No, I don't see why not, you seem a little happier than you have of late.'

'Do I?' That's probably because we had a big breakthrough in the job yesterday,' he replied.

As his office door opened he replaced the telephone handset and said, 'Yes Butcher?'

Butcher informed Alan that there was a General Winters outside his office wanting to speak to him. Alan instructed Butcher to show him in. The General entered the office and without any prompting he introduced himself as being General Winters currently engaged on covert operations, which was a clever way of saying he looked after the Special Air Services. He went on to say; 'Now then, Chief Inspector MacKenzie, I have been asked by the Home Office to assist you in any way that I can.'

Alan replied, 'I take it that you are here in reply to my telephone call yesterday in respect to some weapons we have in our possession.'

The General stated sharply, 'Yes.'

Alan went on to say, 'I believe these weapons belonged to the Army.'

The General replied, 'Yes.'

'So what can you tell me about these weapons?' Alan asked.

The General waited to make his reply as if he had already been scripted as what to say and said, 'I am instructed to tell you that the weapons went missing from Aldershot Barracks about four, nearly five weeks ago.' He again paused and said, 'Quite frankly I am surprised that you managed to identify these items as they belong to the Special Air Services and are supposed to be unidentifiable.'

MacKenzie, realising that he was only going to get out of the General what he had already been instructed to say, then produced the photo-fits of the main suspect to see what reaction he got.

A silence fell upon the office, as the General became lost for words. The silence was broken by a cough as the General cleared his throat, bringing his hand across his mouth at the same time.

'All I can say Chief Inspector is that I do not recognise this person. I can tell you however that he is not a serving member of the SAS. I know all my men,' he said in a clear and menacing tone.

MacKenzie could see that the General was lying, he thought to himself, maybe not lying but being very economical with the truth, which is typical of such an organisation. Alan continued to dig by asking, 'What about past members?'

The General again paused for thought before replying, with

a sharp burst, 'I cannot help you Chief Inspector, I'm sorry but I have another appointment to keep,' and the meeting was concluded.

The General shook MacKenzie's hand and wished him good luck in his enquiry. 'Before you go General, can you tell me anything else about the weapons we recovered?' Alan asked sheepishly.

The General replied, 'No, but I wouldn't waste any time looking at any member of the SAS. You'd be on the wrong track.' He thanked MacKenzie for his time and quickly left the room before Alan could throw another question at him.

Alan muttered to himself that anyone who made a point of saying 'Don't look this way', really meant they were on the right track.

Once the General had left the office Butcher returned. Without wasting his breath MacKenzie instructed Butcher to get in touch with the Home Office, 'I need a list of all known mercenaries, especially those who have had SAS backgrounds,' he said, 'and especially those who have left recently.'

'Yes Sir,' Butcher replied noting the urgency in Alan's voice.

'Butcher,' Alan shouted.

'Yes Sir,' he replied.

'Do it sooner rather than later, we don't want that wily old bird (indicating Winters) getting our man before we do,' he stated.

'I'll do it now Sir,' Butcher replied, as he was leaving the room.

* * *

Paul Lomax attended the usual monthly meeting of the Cabinet. The topic of conversation was of course the drug deaths. Maxwell asked for an update on the numbers of deaths from Joanna Brown. Joanna informed the Cabinet that there had been a slight increase in deaths, which the police felt that was due in some way to the drug dealers off-loading any remaining supply of drugs. 'The figure has actually stopped at around 80,000 countrywide.'

Maxwell said, 'It's unbelievable that someone could do such a thing. Why? That's what I want to know.'

Maxwell looked across to Lomax and asked if he had anything to add.

Lomax coolly and calmly replied, 'Yes. It's been a double-edged sword really. Although we've had all these deaths, in reality the crime rate has actually dropped drastically, especially in respect of burglary, theft and street robberies, by as much as 75 per cent.'

Lomax smiled and added, 'We can't have it both ways. After all the people who have died were only low life spongers anyway. I've no doubt it's had a knock-on effect with the benefit agency.'

Lomax looked across the table at Peter Oncroft, the Benefit Agency Minister.

Oncroft burst into action and said, 'You're quite right, benefit payments are right down and it would appear as if it has reduced benefit fraud as well.'

Joanna interrupted Oncroft. 'That might well be the case but it's hit the health budget really hard, we're well over budget.'

Lomax again stated, 'We can't have it both ways can we?'

Lomax without thinking slipped up and remarked that he had worked hard to get these results.

'What do you mean by that?' Maxwell replied.

'Nothing,' Lomax replied, realising what he had said. 'You wanted the crime figures down, you've got it,' he said trying to get Maxwell's mind off what he had just heard. On completing his speech he slammed his folder shut on the table and smiled at Maxwell.

Maxwell then informed the Cabinet members that the police had a photo-fit of a suspect they were looking for, he then passed a copy of the photo-fit round the table. Maxwell stated that he was not as yet going to the press with this news, and asked all present to keep the news to themselves. 'This is for your interest only.'

When the photo-fit reached Lomax, he coughed and almost choked as the picture resembled Parker. 'What's the matter with you?' Maxwell asked.

'Nothing,' Lomax replied.

After the meeting closed, Lomax became worried. He had no way to contact Parker in order to warn him. The police had done a better job than he had anticipated. Lomax left the meeting and went home.

Joanne Brown turned to Maxwell and said, 'Strange comments from Paul don't you think?'

* * *

It was 21.45 hours on Tuesday, the night sky was clear and the stars shone brightly, the moon was in its full glory, standing proudly illuminating the heavens. It brought with it a brisk, cold wind, which howled around the old barn.

'Is everyone here yet?' Parker asked Evans.

'No Sir, there's still two to come,' he replied.

Parker looked at his watch; its silver face glistened in the moonlight. He looked back at Evans. 'They're leaving it a bit late aren't they?'

Evans didn't reply.

The farmhouse had been unoccupied for about ten years; it had belonged to an old man who was unable to farm the land due to health problems. He eventually had to go into a home, but refused to sell the farm off. The location was ideal for Parker. The farmhouse sat a long way off the main road, down a winding single lane track. The nearest neighbour was two miles away.

The family of Frederick Jones had farmed the land in Norfolk for the past two hundred years. He had wanted to carry on the family tradition, but had a stroke, which rendered him disabled and unable to work. After numerous attempts to get him to sell the property, (he refused hoping that one day he would get better and be able to continue work), the property began to deteriorate. Parker had done his research well.

As the second hand on his watch marched onwards to ten o'clock, Evans announced that the last two of the team had arrived and all were present and correct in the barn.

'OK, I'll be with you shortly,' he replied sternly.

Parker spent an agonising few minutes in deep thought over a decision he had to make.

He whispered to himself, 'Yes', turned and walked off towards the barn.

He entered and saw the team; all of them cheered him as he walked to the centre of the barn. There was a general air of enjoyment.

'Gentlemen!' Parker shouted to be heard over the noise. Suddenly the chanting and cheering stopped as Parker continued; 'I would like to thank all of you, for your hard work and devotion. Without you I couldn't have completed the operation.'

Parker paused. 'Your efforts have brought rewards. Each of you will receive two million pounds sterling.'

On saying that the barn again filled with rapturous applause and cheering.

Evans shouted out, 'Three cheers for Major Parker. Hip Hip.'

'Hooray.'

'Hip Hip.'

'Hooray.'

'Hip Hip.'

'Hooray.'

Parker raised his hand to quieten the mêlée down, 'Thank you all very much, I too must applaud you.'

The room became quiet again as Parker pointed to a crate in the centre of the barn saying, 'In the crate you will find some champagne, help yourselves.'

The boys rushed to open the crate and started to remove bottles of champagne.

'I shall be gone for a short period while I go and get your money,' Parker shouted. He left the barn as all the team gathered round the wooden crate situated in the centre of the room.

Evans looked out of the barn door but could see no signs of Parker; he turned to the men and said, 'I'll go and give him a hand, boys.'

None of the team took any notice as he left; they were too busy removing more bottles of champagne from the crate. They celebrated as champagne corks popped, and then began telling one another what they were going to do with their money.

Evans stopped in his tracks half way across the farmyard, he felt uneasy, something was wrong. He pulled the collar of his coat together around his neck to take away the biting wind, as it seemed to eat its way through him, rather than round him. Evans was about to start off again when suddenly without warning, he was thrown off his feet, crashing to the ground, rolling several times until he came to an abrupt halt against the wall of the farmhouse. He was knocked unconscious as he banged his head against the wall.

Shocked and dazed he began to come round, his senses were confused, and his ears were ringing. He looked in the general direction of the barn. As his eyes began to focus on the barn he could see the roof of the barn was missing and smoke was rising from the building. Holes had appeared in the walls of the barn, which had not been there before and the barn door had been blown off its hinges.

Evans knew an explosion had taken place.

As his senses began to come back he felt severe pain in his left leg; he looked down and saw a large wooden splinter protruding from it. Blood was pouring from the wound. As the pain from the wound began to strike he saw Parker; he appeared from behind the farmhouse. Evans watched as Parker walked quickly across the farmyard towards the barn.

Evans couldn't hear Parker's footsteps as he was still deafened from the explosion. He watched quietly as Parker entered the barn.

Evans' mind was working overtime. It appeared to him that Parker had expected the explosion. 'Bastard,' he muttered to himself. 'He's planned it.'

Evans thought quickly, thinking to himself that he had better move out of sight, in case Parker found him and finished him off as well.

Parker entered the barn. There was a huge hole in the ground where the wooden champagne crate had stood; mutilated, charred bodies were lying all around. Parker attempted to count the bodies, but he couldn't. He was surprised that the impact of the explosion had caused so much damage. He thought to himself, 'Maybe I used too many explosives, but there again I didn't want anyone to survive.'

He looked round the barn, 'No, they're all dead,' he muttered. He didn't stay to take a count.

The Police Operations Room at the Norfolk Constabulary Headquarters suddenly began to get busy. The lights on the telephone exchange began to flicker as a number of telephone calls were received reporting the sound of a large explosion in the area of Jones' farm.

'Excuse me Sir,' the operator said to the Duty Inspector. 'It would appear as if some sort of incident has occurred near to Jones' farm, there are reports of an explosion.'

The Inspector replied, 'You'd better send some patrols over there to see what's going on.'

'OK Sir,' the operator said as he picked up the radio control.

'What about the helicopter?' the Inspector asked.

'Still out of commission, Sir, until tomorrow,' was the reply.

'Typical,' he muttered, 'just when you need it.'

Evans was in great pain now, but he crawled along the ground and into an outbuilding, out of Parker's way. He knew he was in no fit state to take Parker on. In the distance Parker could hear the sound of two-tone sirens, it seemed to jolt Parker into action as he quickly left the barn. On leaving he looked round ensuring there was nothing obvious to link the explosion with him.

Evans observed as Parker's pace quickened, he watched as Parker left the barn, entered the farmhouse and then left. He swore as he saw him get into a vehicle and drive away as if nothing had happened.

Evans looked at his leg, he saw that his trouser leg was covered in blood. He took hold of the splinter with both hands, took a deep breath and yanked the splinter sharply from his leg. He yelled out in pain as it was plucked from his flesh. He pulled himself up and limped across the farmyard, dragging his injured leg. He fell against the remains of the door of the barn and looked inside.

Hardened to battle conditions as he was, tears flooded into his eyes, They were all friends. 'Now they're all dead,' he muttered. 'Bastard,' he shouted.

As the police sirens began to get louder Evans made his way to his vehicle, climbed in and drove away.

He gazed into his rear view mirror, frowned and said; 'I'll get the bastard for you boys.'

CHAPTER NINE

It was 5 a.m. the next day when the first police vehicle drove along the single lane track to Jones' farm. The officer driving was taking his time, as the morning frost had frozen small pools of water. The crisp sound of the ice cracking could clearly be heard as the car tyres drove across them.

As they approached the farmhouse and outbuildings, it was clear to the police officers that they had found the location they had been looking for over the past several hours.

'Tango four zero to XH,' the officer said on his radio.

'Go ahead tango four zero,' was the reply.

'From tango four zero, it would appear as if we have found the location, we will give you a Sit-Rep as soon as possible.'

The two officers got out from the police vehicle and began a steady approach towards the barn. It was clear to them that the barn had been the site of the explosion.

The scene was eerie. The air was calm and cold and steam could be seen coming out of the officers' mouths as hot breath met cool air every time they exhaled.

'Careful Charlie,' one officer said to the other, as they reached the barn doors.

Police Constable 1025 Charlie Williams was the first officer to enter the scene.

'Bloody Hell,' he shouted to his mate, who had just at that moment entered the barn. As the second officer gazed at the sight before him, he suddenly felt sick and rushed from the barn and began to vomit outside.

Charlie Williams took a sharp deep breath and slowly exhaled. His hand slowly reached up to his radio button, which he pressed with his now trembling thumb, not sure if it was shock or the cold causing him to shake.

'Tango four zero to XH,' he said.

'Tango four zero go ahead,' came the reply.

'From tango four zero, we do have an incident at this location, I will require Detective supervision, Scenes of Crime and I will commence a major incident log.'

The operator replied, 'Tango four zero received, can you ascertain what has taken place at the location?'

'From tango four zero, there has been some kind of explosion at this location, there are a number of persons dead, about twenty bodies in total.'

There was a slight pause, the radio crackled, 'Tango four zero received.'

Within the next couple of hours the Norfolk Constabulary Major Incident Team sprang into action.

* * *

Alan MacKenzie's day began as usual; he attended the morning's briefing. The main question on his mind was what developments there had been regarding the mercenary enquiry which he had asked Butcher to make with the Home Office. Butcher informed MacKenzie that an appointment had been made with the Defence Minister, Alan Cartwright, for eleven that morning.

Paul Lomax was sitting at his office desk on the telephone when Helen entered the office carrying the morning's post. She placed the mail into his tray and overheard his conversation. 'Once again Alan, thank you for calling, but I think that in the interest of National Security that information should be withheld.'

Paul then replaced the receiver and said, 'Thank you Helen.'

Helen replied, 'Was that Alan MacKenzie?' in an enquiring way.

'Good heavens no, Alan Cartwright, he sends you his regards.'

'Oh how nice,' she replied as she left the office.

Butcher arrived at the Ministry of Defence building at ten forty-five. He was directed to the third floor and situated at the end of a very long corridor was the Minister's office. Butcher thought to himself that the location of the office reminded him of an advertisement he had seen on television about the complaints department of a well-known beer. He was shown into a poky little room which appeared to be a leftover from the nineteen sixties, and hardly used.

Alan Cartwright was every bit a 'civil servant', polite, smartly dressed and not very forthcoming with information. He had been previously warned of the purpose of Butcher's visit.

Cartwright informed Butcher that he was unable to furnish the information he required as it was a matter of national security and any information in respect of members of the SAS, serving or past members was highly classified.

Butcher impressed on the Minister of the urgency of the request. Cartwright brushed his request aside saying, 'Again, Mr Butcher, I am unable to assist your enquiries as I said before this information is classified.'

Butcher left the Defence Department building at eleven thirty, cursing himself as he had been unable to glean any information. 'MacKenzie will be furious,' he mumbled. 'He will not be a happy man.'

On his arrival back at the office Butcher immediately went to update MacKenzie. Within seconds of the meeting, others outside the office could clearly hear MacKenzie shout a loud, 'You what!'

Alan didn't lose his temper often, but when he did everyone knew it was time to stay away. The offices cleared very quickly. The telephone rang in his office; still annoyed he answered it and shouted, 'What!'

'Oh, it would appear as if I have caught you at the wrong time,' a calming voice said.

'Sorry darling, you did catch me at a bad time, that's all,' he replied.

'Shall I ring back later?' she asked.

Alan calmed down and had a five-minute conversation with her.

He had to decline a night out as he was appearing on the BBC Crimewatch programme. She chuckled and said, 'I'd better not miss that programme then had I? Do you want me to tape it for you?'

'I don't think so', laughing as he said so.

* * *

Evans had returned to his flat situated on the South Shore area of Blackpool. He was weak and tired. He stripped off and examined his leg wound. He found it to be still bleeding quite heavily. He knew he had lost a lot of blood and that the injury required stitches. He thought that he couldn't risk going to the hospital for treatment and so removed a survival first aid kit from his kit bag.

Evans removed from the first aid kit a needle and thread. He then injected a mild sedative into his leg and began to sew the parting flesh together. The bleeding began to stop, and although he was in extreme pain, he managed to place a clean white bandage around his leg just before he passed out.

Several hours later, still in considerable pain, he regained his senses, and he made the decision to rest for the rest of the day before planning his revenge on Parker.

* * *

At 6 p.m. MacKenzie arrived at the BBC Television Studio where he was to take part in the BBC Crimewatch programme. He had had an exhausting day of meetings following Butcher's revelations that the Home Office was refusing to help in the enquiry.

The day had begun with a meeting with the Chief Constable. Sir Peter Ashbourne wasn't very happy either and stated that he was under the impression from the Prime Minister that no obstacles would be in the way.

That meeting led to another meeting with himself, the Chief and the Commissioner, who, as it was thought, took the middle road stating that he could understand both sides of the argument. That meeting ended with the Commissioner saying that he would raise the matter at the next day's meeting with the PM.

Alan forgetting himself again, said to the Commissioner 'That's all very well Sir, but that's another day wasted because of red tape.'

Both the Commissioner and the Chief looked at Alan not saying a word. Alan knew from the silence that he had overstepped the mark.

Without anything else being spoken MacKenzie said 'Thank you for your time, Sir', turned and walked away. As he walked along the corridor he could hear the Commissioner and the Chief mumbling to each other.

Alan was shown to the room where the television programme was to be produced. He was amazed at just how small the studio was and thought to himself that it appeared larger on the television. He was greeted by Nick Ross and informed of the itinerary.

Following a dress rehearsal that resulted in Alan stuttering his words, Nick Ross told him not to worry and that it wouldn't happen when the programme started for real. 'I hope not,' Alan said as he rose from his seat and was guided by an extremely attractive young lady to the make up department.

The programme commenced right on time at ten p.m. and at ten twenty p.m., bang on schedule, came Alan's spot. Nick Ross started by announcing, 'Now here we have something which has affected most of the country, the murder of thousands of people.'

Alan knew the reason as to why the enquiry was not featured first on the programme; it was because of the type of people that were the victims, drug takers. It was a general feeling by the programme makers that a lot of people wouldn't have much sympathy towards them.

Alan thought differently to this, as from an early age he was taught the family was always put first, for every one who has died was someone's son or daughter.

Helen was sat at home watching the television when at ten p.m. she turned channels to the BBC to watch Crimewatch. At the same time she started the video recorder and began taping the same programme.

She watched Alan as he delivered his speech. She thought to herself how caring he had come across on the television. Her thoughts wandered away from the television and she began thinking of Alan. 'That's the man I want to spend the rest of my life with,' she found herself saying out loud as reality set in when a computer-compiled picture was shown on the screen of the main suspect in the enquiry.

Suddenly she shouted, 'Oh my god', realising the link between Paul Lomax and Major Parker. 'Bloody hell', she said as she recalled the time when Lomax borrowed her laptop.

As soon as Alan finished his spot he could hear the telephone calls being answered. Nick Ross took hold of Alan by the arm and said, 'Well done'. Nick smiled and turned away to read his next part of the programme.

Helen went to bed but couldn't sleep and spent the night tossing and turning.

* * *

Alan left the BBC studio at two a.m. There had been thousands of calls as a result of his appeal, the phones closed at midnight.

The Crimewatch crew and the teams of Police Officers went for a farewell drink after the programme. Alan arrived home at three a.m. and crashed out exhausted on his bed fully clothed.

Parker was staying at the London Hilton Hotel. He too watched the Crimewatch programme and he too recognised the computerised photograph of the suspect as resembling him. Instinctively he rushed into the hotel bathroom, where he shaved off his moustache and gave his head a number two shave. He looked in the mirror and began thinking how the police had managed to get a likeness of him.

At first he thought of Lomax but immediately discounted this because he was just as much involved as he was. Parker spent the rest of the night in deep thought retracing his steps from the day he met Lomax.

CHAPTER TEN

The day began early for Helen as she rushed into her office. She removed her office keys from her handbag and due to her rushing, she dropped the keys onto the floor. 'Damn,' she shouted to herself.

She fumbled as she inserted the keys into the bottom drawer of her desk and turned the key. She paused for thought. 'Do I really want to know?' Her curiosity got the better of her as she quickly opened the drawer before she changed her mind; she removed a blank folder and began reading its contents.

Dismayed by what she was reading, she muttered 'Oh why didn't you read this before, you stupid, stupid bitch.' She began feeling sick.

Helen placed the folder into her handbag and walked out of the office informing her junior that she was feeling unwell, and was going home. Mandy the office junior was gob-smacked, as in the past ten years she had worked with Helen, she had never known her to be off work sick before.

Helen returned home where she locked and bolted the door, feeling guilty about removing a file from the office and fearing that someone may have seen her. She looked out of the window checking that she hadn't been followed. The fears she was having were only in her mind and it took at least three hours for those feelings to subside. When she felt safe again she removed the blank folder from her bag and began to read its contents again, more slowly this time, digesting every word, every paragraph, every page.

Just as Helen was about to conclude the last page, the telephone rang; it startled her making her jump. She picked the receiver up and answered, 'Yes'.

'Helen?' her heart missed a beat and she began to sweat. 'It's me Paul, just ringing to see how you are.'

She hesitated before answering, 'I'll, I'll be alright soon, Paul. I'm, I'm not feeling too well at the moment.'

'Well listen, don't rush back too soon, get yourself better first,' he told her.

She replaced the telephone in panic and walked across the lounge where she picked up a bottle and poured herself a triple brandy. She was at a loss as to what to do with the file and so pulled the carpet back in her bedroom and placed the folder underneath.

* * *

Alan MacKenzie began his day by analysing the results from the Crimewatch programme. There had been thousands of telephone calls as a result of his appeal.

He informed Butcher that a couple of members from the team would have to go through all the calls and place them into some sort of priority. Privately Alan didn't put much focus on the information but knew that every line of enquiry would have to be followed up as the enquiry went on.

By mid afternoon the same day Butcher received a telephone call from the Forensic Science Laboratory.

A young man on the other end of the line announced himself and said, 'I have a message for Chief Inspector MacKenzie. We have a hit on the DNA sample he has an interest in and could he contact Professor Armstrong at his convenience.'

Butcher tried to enquire further but the young man stated that he himself had no further information and put the telephone down. Butcher sprang from his chair pushing it backwards, causing it to fall over in his rush. He entered MacKenzie's office without knocking.

'Boss,' he shouted.

'What's the matter with you?' Alan enquired.

'We've had a call from the lab, there's a hit on the DNA,' Butcher said excitedly.

'Is there?' Alan said, so matter of factly that Butcher was quite taken aback. Little did he know that MacKenzie was just as excited but didn't want to show it.

'Well who is it then?' Alan asked.

'I don't know,' Butcher replied.

'What do you mean you don't know?'

'They wouldn't tell me, the message was could you contact Professor Armstrong at the lab,' Butcher said almost as an instruction.

'Thank you,' Alan said.

Butcher didn't know what to do, he saw MacKenzie look down at his desk and continue with what he was doing. He shook his head and turned away. Alan glanced up, looked at Butcher and smiled to himself. Butcher left the office. Once the door closed behind him, Alan picked the telephone up and rang the lab.

'Professor Armstrong please.'

'Who's calling?' the lady receptionist enquired.

'Yes, it's Chief Inspector MacKenzie, returning his call.'

'Oh yes, Professor Armstrong is expecting your call,' she replied.

'I bet he is,' Alan thought to himself.

'Hello Alan, thanks for calling back. Your DNA sample has come back with a hit.'

'So I understand.'

The Professor continued, 'The Police in Norfolk are dealing with an explosion at one of their isolated farmhouses where a number of people were killed.'

'Yes,' Alan said slowly.

'Because of problems they were having with identifying those killed, we were asked to do DNA profiles and one of them comes back to a hit on your enquiry.'

'Is that a positive hit or a maybe?' Alan said hoping for a positive.

'Positive, without any doubt; we still don't know who he is mind you, but at least you know where he is.'

Alan's conversation with Armstrong lasted another half an hour, during which Butcher entered the office at least five times, obviously wanting to know more about the call. Eventually Alan ended his call.

'Butcher,' Alan shouted. As soon as he called, the office door opened as if he was stood outside.

'We're off to Norfolk,' Alan said without further ado.

'Are we boss, what's happened?' Butcher enquired.

'It would appear as if our boy has turned up in Norfolk, dead unfortunately. I'll tell you more on the way.'

It took only half an hour for the two to be setting off to Norfolk. Four hours later they arrived at the County Police Headquarters where Alan announced himself to the Enquiry Office clerk.

'Is the Superintendent expecting you Sir?' the clerk enquired.

'I don't think so, I didn't have time to arrange anything.'

'He's very busy Sir, he might not be in, I'll just try for you.' The clerk dialled the extension number and after a short conversation said, 'OK Sir, straight away.'

Alan was allowed entry and was shown to the CID office where he was introduced to Superintendent Stevens.

After their initial conversation Superintendent Stevens said, 'Bloody hell, I take it from that you wish to take this enquiry over?'

'Not at all, we don't have the resources to do that, but your enquiry will become an important part of ours. Tell me what you've got.'

Stevens walked MacKenzie and Butcher to the Incident Room and began bringing them up to speed with the enquiry.

'Do we know who they are?' Alan asked.

'We haven't got a clue,' Stevens replied.

As the hours passed Alan decided that they would have to stay the night in Norfolk. Arrangements were made for them to stay in a local hotel for the night. Alan arranged with Stevens that he be allowed to visit the farmhouse and look at the exhibits the following day.

Helen kept ringing Alan's home telephone number but all she could get was his answer machine. She had already left several messages on it and on subsequent calls she just slammed the phone down in frustration. 'Where the hell are you Alan?' she muttered.

It just so happened that when Alan rushed out of the office he left his mobile phone on his desk. Again Helen had left several messages on the answering service.

'It's bloody typical when you want someone they're never around,' she said angrily.

Alan spent a quiet night on the town being entertained by the local CID and managed to get to bed at around one a.m. He was up ready and raring to go at seven thirty a.m. the same day. Butcher, having consumed a little more alcohol than Alan the night before, arrived at breakfast late, a little the worse for wear.

'Is it good morning or not?' Alan asked with a grin.

'I haven't yet decided boss,' he muttered in reply.

At nine o'clock MacKenzie attended the morning briefing. There was murmuring in the briefing room wondering who he was and what MacKenzie was doing there. All was revealed and an air of excitement rang round the room similar to that which first greeted Alan's team on learning the facts of the case.

MacKenzie and Butcher spent the rest of the day visiting the scene of the explosion, the mortuary and looking through exhibits. Alan could find nothing of significance except one thing common to all the deceased; they were fairly young, muscular fit-looking people. This puzzled him a bit.

'One thing, are there any drugs involved?' Alan asked.

'Well that posed us a question. All the exhibits had traces of heroin, and we found a number of emptied drums of poison,' Stevens replied.

'I haven't seen those,' Alan stated.

'No you haven't, because they were sent to the lab for examination and we don't have a result as yet,' Stevens replied.

MacKenzie left Stevens, thanking him for his assistance and requesting that he be briefed of any developments as they occurred. He spent a period of quiet contemplation on his journey back to London. He wondered to himself, 'Did my man kill himself in the explosion or did he cause it? Was the man callous enough to kill his mates?'

On his return to London Alan told Butcher to get in touch with the lab about the canisters of poison, 'I would like to know where they had come from.'

Once Butcher had left the office Alan finally called his girlfriend. 'Hi,' he said when he got a reply.

'Where the hell have you been, I've been trying to get hold of you for ages?' she replied.

'Hold on, calm down, what's the matter?'

'I need to see you, can I see you tonight,' she asked.

Alan agreed without any hesitation. He returned home at six thirty that evening and after having a quick bite to eat, he showered and changed, then waited for his guest to arrive.

Alan felt uneasy. He had an uncanny feeling, which caused the hairs on the back of his neck to stand on end. He actually thought someone had been following him. He brushed his thoughts aside thinking that maybe it had something to do with his earlier phone call. At seven thirty his doorbell rang.

In the carpark facing the front of the flats where Alan lived, was parked a motor vehicle. A lone man sat inside keeping observation on Alan's flat. A number of cigarette ends lay on the ground near to the driver's door. The vehicle had been there for a few hours, since Alan returned home. It was Parker.

Parker had used the time between Alan returning home and his girlfriend arriving to survey the premises. He had memorised every exit point and escape route if he required one. Parker waited and waited.

Helen couldn't settle and she explained to Alan that she had a problem at work, which she didn't know what to do about. Alan asked what it was but all she would say was that it came under the Official Secrets Act and she couldn't say.

Alan got slightly annoyed and said, 'What the hell are you worried about then, if you can't tell anyone, forget it, why worry?'

'It's easy for you to say,' she replied as she poured herself a third brandy, 'I've been looking over my shoulder ever since I found out.'

'Well what is it?' he again asked.

Again she refused to say as she gulped the third brandy down.

'What you need is a bit of TLC,' Alan said as he took hold of her and cuddled her tightly.

'I'm sorry Alan,' she said with tears in her eyes.

Alan kissed her, then paused, he held her head in both hands and looked straight into her eyes. He kissed her again, then paused again and looked her straight in her eyes.

He did it a third time, to which she responded by passionately grabbing hold of his hair and pulling him forward and kissing him. She started to undo his shirt buttons and without trying, Alan appeared to be getting pushed backwards and he fell onto the settee. She pulled his shirt open and immediately unbuttoned her blouse and rubbed her breasts on Alan's chest.

Alan responded by slipping her blouse off her shoulders and began caressing her back with his fingers. They rolled onto the floor and began removing each other's lower garments. Alan paused on top of her, muttered the words, 'Darling I love you.' He entered her as her whole body raised with pleasure.

Helen forgot her worries for a while as she made love to the man she had decided to give her love to.

Tears again appeared in her eyes and Alan said, 'Are you alright darling?'

She smiled, and quietly and passionately replied, 'Yes.'

After making love they laid for a while without speaking, reeling in the pleasures of sex, both being on a high.

Suddenly without any warning they both became aware of another person's presence in the room.

Alan turned round and saw a man dressed all in black, holding what appeared to be an automatic pistol in his hand. The gun was pointed at Alan's head. 'Don't move, and you won't get hurt,' Parker shouted.

'What the hell?' Alan shouted in panic.

Parker threw Alan a roll of tape and instructed Alan to bind Helen's hands and feet.

'Let her get dressed first,' Alan shouted.

'No time for that,' Parker said as he quickly took his eyes off Alan to gaze at Helen's naked form.

'Do it now,' Parker shouted.

'Sorry darling,' Alan whispered as he began to place the tape around her wrist.

'Behind her back,' Parker shouted.

Helen placed her hands behind her back and Alan bound them together loosely. He did the same with her feet.

Parker then instructed Alan to place his hands behind his back, he complied and Parker collected the roll of tape and bound Alan's hands up very tightly. He then did the same with his feet.

After doing so Parker redid Helen's hands and feet. He looked at her and said, 'Sorry little lady, but needs must.'

Parker looked at Helen momentarily thinking to himself, I know you from somewhere.

He said to her, 'Where do I know you from?'

She replied, 'I've never seen you before in my life,' but fear could be seen on her face.

She was lying of course, she recalled full well where she had seen him, in Lomax's office. Major Parker.

Helen was frightened and tears began streaming down her face, thinking that if Parker recognised her that she'd be killed. She turned her head away in an attempt to make it more difficult for Parker to recognise her.

'Chief Inspector MacKenzie,' Parker said.

'You've got me at a disadvantage,' Alan replied. 'I know the face, but not the name.'

Alan knew that the man before him was the person the photo-fit fitted and that both Helen and he were in danger.

Alan also knew that the intruder had managed to enter his flat while he and Helen had been making love, and that was why he failed to hear him enter the room. He shuddered to think what he saw and at what time he had entered the flat. Alan's thoughts soon came back to the danger he and Helen were in.

'What do you want?' Alan asked.

'So you don't know who I am?' he laughed and said, 'The Government are not telling you everything then, Mr MacKenzie?'

'Why are you here?' Alan asked.

'I am here to warn you off, Mr Policeman. You have done a good job, but leave it alone, you don't know what you have got involved in,' came the reply.

'I do not understand, why put yourself at risk coming here, what's the point to all this?' Alan asked.

'I have come to warn you that this thing is far bigger than you or I, and to tell you to leave it alone.'

'What about those you killed in Norfolk?' Alan asked.

'You're good. I didn't think you would have connected that yet,' Parker replied.

He paused, as he looked Helen up and down. He smiled and said, 'It was part of my brief that no one would be left but me and my employer.'

'And what about us?' Alan asked.

'I will not kill you yet, but if you come too close I cannot make any guarantees. Leave it alone, Policeman, there are people involved far greater than you and me. Understand?' Parker waved his gun at Alan.

'Time for me to go,' Parker said.

Before leaving, Parker sat Helen and Alan against a dining chair and bound them to it with tape. 'Sorry about this but I need time to get away.'

'Let the lady get dressed first,' Alan pleaded.

'Sorry,' was the reply.

Helen said nothing throughout the ordeal; frightened that Parker would recognise her. Once he had gone she shouted at Alan, 'What are we going to do?'

Alan tried to get loose from the binding but couldn't. 'We're going to have to wait,' he said.

Helen was not amused, as she lay naked and helpless.

'Why do you think he said that he thought he knew you?' Alan asked Helen.

'What? I don't know,'

Helen tried to change the subject, 'Alan, get us out of this.'

'Strange,' was his reply, 'I can't.'

At nine a.m. the following morning, the telephone rang at Alan's flat and the answer machine came on. It was Butcher enquiring where he was. Alan swore and muttered, 'Get yourself over here.'

That morning Butcher was busy with the Forensic Lab and he requested uniform to send someone round to Alan's flat to see everything was in order. It was unusual for Alan not to answer his phones or to say where he could be contacted, especially if he was going to be late for work.

At eleven o' clock two female Police Officers arrived at Alan's front door. They found that the door had been left ajar. Before entering they removed their ASP Batons, extended them and then slowly opened the door to the flat.

'Police, anyone here?' one of the Police Officers shouted.

'We're in here,' Alan shouted back.

The Policewomen entered the room and found themselves confronted by a naked Chief Inspector and a naked woman bound to dining chairs.

'Are you alright Sir?' one of them asked.

'Yes. Just get us free,' Alan requested.

'Do her first,' he instructed them.

The Policewomen released Helen first and then began to release Alan. He was embarrassed as he bared all he possessed to the Policewomen; he got up and quickly slipped some clothes on.

'Is there anything I should know, Sir?' the Policewoman asked, trying not to smirk.

'No,' Alan replied.

'What shall I put in my report, Sir?' She smiled and completed her sentence, 'Was it some fantasy that went wrong, Sir?'

'Get out, I'll clear the log report,' he shouted back rudely.

'Yes Sir,' they replied as they left the flat giggling like two young schoolchildren.

'I'm very sorry darling, what can I say,' Alan said.

'It's not your fault is it, how are you going to live this down at the nick?' she asked.

Alan knew before Helen said anything that he would be the subject of ridicule when he got back to the station. After ringing Butcher he drove Helen home and left her on the doorstep.

Alan could see that she was very worried about something and he left her saying, 'It'll be alright'.

'I know,' she said confidently.

CHAPTER ELEVEN

On entering her flat Helen showered. She felt dirty, the fact that some other man had violated her space and viewed her naked body, without her consent, and not only Parker but the two unknown Policewomen, sickened her. She thought, even worse she could be dead now, if Parker had recognised her. This really made her sick and she rushed off to the bathroom, where she vomited violently.

She washed her face, dried it and sat sipping a cup of tea, wrapped in a crisp white dressing gown. Helen thought long and deep. Did Parker recognise her? If not, how long would it be before he recalled her? Then she thought, 'He had only seen me for a few minutes, he won't remember me'.

She began to panic. 'If he could get into Alan's home, what chance have I?' she whispered to herself.

Helen left for the office and walked straight to her desk. She removed from her handbag a brown envelope and removed its contents. She called for Mandy, her office junior. 'I want you to do me an errand, please.'

'Are you alright?' asked Mandy, 'I've never known you like this, coming to work late, and taking time off sick, has something happened?'

'No I'm fine,' Helen replied, brushing off her worried look.

Helen scribbled Paul Lomax's name on the paperwork, indicating that he was the author of the report and replaced the papers.

'Now. I would like you to hand deliver this envelope to Chief

Inspector Alan MacKenzie at New Scotland Yard.' As she was saying this Helen was writing in big bold letters Alan's name and title, finishing with the words Private and Confidential. She then placed sellotape around the seals of the envelope and handed it to Mandy.

'Right then, off you go and don't lose the envelope whatever you do.'

Helen watched in silence as Mandy left the office. She was in a momentary trance, which was suddenly interrupted by Lomax entering the office.

MacKenzie arrived at the office about noon; he had his angry head on. As he entered the CID Department he found it to be empty.

Word of what had happened had already filtered back to the investigating team and it was wise for them to be missing for a while. They knew what Alan was going to be like.

As he reached his office door he found that someone was brave enough to affix to the door a doodle and a message indicating where Alan could find fetish equipment. He tore it from the door, entered the office and slammed the door shut.

Butcher knocked and entered the office; Alan placed the doodle into Butcher's top pocket. He removed it and glanced at the contents. 'Well what do you expect?' he said.

Alan raised a single finger in Butcher's direction indicating to Butcher to say no more.

'What is worrying about all this Butcher, is the fact that this man could have killed us both. I intend to get this bastard,' Alan shouted.

'Give me half an hour to calm down and get the team together for a briefing,' he added.

Butcher left the office and returned a few minutes later with a hot cup of tea; 'I have some news for you when you're ready boss.'

'Come and see me before the briefing,' Alan suggested.

Twenty-five minutes later Butcher returned to Alan's office and updated him about the enquiries into the poison recovered in Norfolk.

'Well Sir, it would appear that the poison was from the Brents Pharmacy Distribution warehouse in Nottingham. It appears that the serial numbers on the poison drums could be traced back to them. Also the poison is a match to ours.'

'Why didn't they come forward with this information first?' Alan asked.

'It appears that it was embarrassing to the company and that they had their own investigators on it,' he replied.

'What have we got from them then?' Alan enquired.

'The description of the person collecting the consignment matches those which the Catterick officers gave us,' Butcher replied.

'Well that's good then, at least things are coming together a little,' Alan replied.

The two trotted into the briefing, the room was silent when they entered.

Alan began by saying to the gathering; 'Well at least we know this bastard is still alive.'

On saying this, the whole room burst out with laughter. Even the Chief had a smile on his face. It was unusual for the Chief to attend the meetings but on this occasion he too had something to offer the briefing.

The Chief informed the gathering that he had at last obtained from the Ministry of Defence a comprehensive list of SAS members, old and new. 'They have boxed clever of course, by providing us with a list going back to when they first set up, during the last war.'

Alan enquired, 'Why is that then, what interest have they got in this enquiry?'

The Chief replied, 'I can only assume that if it was one of theirs – even ex-members, that Department's going to come under severe examination in any public enquiry.'

'I fear that in this case they would rather get hold of this man before we do,' Alan suggested.

A firm 'Yes,' came back from the Chief.

After the briefing the Chief and Alan returned to his office. The Chief enquired if Alan was all right. Alan assured him that he was and they continued to discuss the case.

'What I cannot understand is, why he didn't kill us? And who was he talking about, people far bigger than him or us were involved?'

The Chief stated he didn't know and that they would have to find that out to find the answer to everything that had happened. 'In respect to not killing you,' he added, 'I believe he may need an ally if things go wrong for him. Mind you I'm glad he didn't kill you.'

'Thanks,' Alan said. 'So am I.'

Alan spent the rest of the day examining the list from the MOD; there were hundreds of names. He gave it to Butcher and said, 'We'll have to find a way of reducing this list, Frank.'

'Well that's easy boss, quite a few of these will be dead or too old, especially those from the war,' he said.

Alan replied, 'Yes of course, I'm not thinking straight.'

Butcher suggested that Alan should go home. Alan told him that he was moving into one of the Section houses for the time being as his flat was not safe until Parker was caught.

Alan left the office. He kept telling himself that he should ring his girlfriend, but he kept thinking that by now she had time to think about what had happened and would be annoyed. He didn't want to say anything that would upset their relationship. So he didn't bother. He returned home, packed a suitcase then left for the Hendon Police College where he had managed to obtain a room. He lay on the bed looking up at the ceiling, and without knowing, fell into a deep sleep.

* * *

A young attractive female entered the foyer of the New Scotland Yard offices; she approached the enquiry counter desk. The two male employees there fought to see to the lady first. 'Can I help you?' one of them said.

'Yes I have an envelope here for Detective Chief Inspector Alan MacKenzie,' she said in a strong clear voice.

The counter clerk telephoned the CID office and spoke to Butcher. After a short conversation Butcher said that he'd pop down to see her. The counter clerk turned and looked at Mandy, saying, 'Someone's coming down to see you Miss.'

The young female went and sat down on some seats in the foyer and tried to pull her skirt down slightly before she sat down.

The two men in the office watched as she sat. She crossed her legs and showed a considerable amount of thigh. She glanced across to the enquiry desk, which caused the two men to suddenly look away from her direction to avoid embarrassment.

Butcher entered the office, 'Which one is it?' he enquired.

'Guess,' the reply came with a smile on their faces.

'How does he do it, he gets all the luck,' Frank retorted.

Butcher entered the foyer. 'Hello Miss. I'm sorry but Chief Inspector MacKenzie has gone home for the day, can I help you?'

She stated, 'I have a personal package for him.'

'Well, can I take it?'

'Only if you can assure me that (a), he gets it and (b), no one else reads it,' she looked straight into Butcher's eyes.

He stuttered, 'Yes I can ensure that.'

'You look trustworthy,' she said as she uncrossed her legs exposing a glimpse of red knickers. She stood up and handed Butcher the envelope.

'Thank you, may I say who it's from?'

'Sorry I cannot say.' She left the building as Butcher watched her, hardly taking his eyes off her until she disappeared out of view.

He turned towards the enquiry desk and gestured, 'Wow'.

Butcher saw that the envelope was marked 'private and confidential', so he returned to Alan's office and placed it into his tray, unopened.

Mandy returned, and Helen asked, 'Did you deliver it?'

Mandy replied, 'He wasn't in so I left it with a Sergeant Butcher.

Helen was quite happy with that, as she had heard of his name. Alan thought highly of him.

'Did he say where the Chief Inspector was?' she asked.

'No they said he had gone home for the day.'

Helen picked up the telephone and rang Alan's number; there was no reply.

Helen left the office at 5 p.m. For the first time in her life she began to fear going home. When she got there she switched every light on in the house and looked in every room, including the wardrobe.

At 7 p.m. Alan picked up the courage to ring her. He found her to be in a good mood, considering the ordeal he had put her through. Little did he know she was in as much danger as he was. They agreed that both of them needed an early night. They decided not to see each other that day.

Before leaving the office Butcher made a telephone call to an old mate of his, Peter Mann. Peter Mann had been to university with Frank and they arranged to meet later that night at the Light Dragoon public house, off the Edgware Road.

* * *

Parker was in his hotel room when the telephone rang. He picked the receiver up and answered it, saying, 'Yes.'

'You bastard,' was the reply.

Parker knew immediately who the voice belonged to. There was a deathly pause as he quickly gained his thoughts.

'Evans, thank god you're OK,' Parker said. 'I thought you were all dead.'

'I know you do.'

'What happened in the barn?' Parker enquired.

'Don't fucking give me that you bastard, you killed them all, I saw you,' Evans shouted down the phone.

'No you've got it all wrong mate, it wasn't me. After I heard the explosion, I came back and you were all dead – well I thought you were,' Parker explained.

'We need to talk, I'll ring tomorrow at three, I'll give you the location then.' Evans replaced the receiver.

'Shit!' Parker shouted. He knew he now had a problem – how to get rid of Evans. It was not going to be easy as Evans was a master of planning. Now he was in his hands, a position Parker did not like. A restless night lay ahead for him.

* * *

Butcher waited in the public house until Peter arrived, he was late and apologised to Frank. 'Oh don't worry yourself, let me get you a drink.'

'I'll have a pint if you don't mind.' Peter replied.

Frank returned with a headless pint of 'Brewers droop' beer and handed it to Peter. 'Thanks'. He took hold of the glass from Frank and quickly sipped from it.

'It seemed quite urgent when you rang, is there a problem?' Peter enquired.

'We've helped each other out in the past, yes?'

'Yes,' Peter replied in anticipation.

Frank then began telling Peter a story about the SAS link in the enquiry and Winters' involvement. At the end of this, Peter said, 'I don't really think I can help you except that the Hilton Hotel has been a focus of a lot of attention at the moment, and I think there is some kind of operation planned for tomorrow.'

'Do you know what it's all about?'

'No I don't, but General Winters is overseeing the operation personally,' Peter said in a whisper.

'Do you know any details?' Frank enquired.

'No but I can find out. I could lose my job over this Frank.'

'Only if they find out. Don't forget I've stretched my neck out for you over the years Pete,' Frank retorted.

'I'll give you a ring tomorrow. Anyway enough of work, cheers,' Peter then gulped the rest of the pint down. 'Another?'

Frank nodded his head and Pete nipped off to the bar.

Peter Mann, on leaving University had joined the Army, leaving after seven years, when he gained employment with the Ministry of Defence, Special Services Department. He had access to highly sensitive material.

It was a restless night for all; Helen found she could not sleep, Alan had slept earlier and couldn't sleep. Butcher was wondering what Winters was up to.

Alan was up early and went down for breakfast. He had a fat man's helping of eggs, bacon, tomato and hash browns, swilled down by a pint mug of tea.

He rose and left for work arriving in the office at 7.30 a.m.

He casually picked up a large brown envelope from his in tray and opened it; the envelope was marked 'private and confidential'.

He removed the contents and saw it contained a bundle of

papers, which started with the words FOR YOUR EYES ONLY.

Alan threw the papers onto the desk, then glanced through his in tray to see what else of interest was there for him to look at.

At that point Butcher entered the office and informed him of his meeting with an informant, which took Alan's interest. 'What's Winters up to then?'

'I don't know Sir, but I'm getting a call later today from the source.'

'Frank you'd better get a guest list of people staying at the Hilton while you're at it.'

'OK boss,' Frank replied as he left the office.

'Today is going to be a good day,' Alan muttered to himself.

He sat and began reading the contents of his package and saw the name Paul Lomax which drew his attention.

As he read he became even more involved in its content. 'Fucking hell!' he said just as Butcher entered the office.

'Briefing time boss,' Frank reminded him.

'Delay it for an hour, can you Frank?'

'Yes boss, if that's what you want,' Frank walked away.

'Shut the door,' Alan shouted as he continued to read.

'Fucking hell,' he shouted again.

Forty minutes later he had read the contents twice over from cover to cover.

'Butcher,' he shouted. Frank rushed into the office. 'Yes boss?'

'Where did this come from?' holding up the brown envelope.

'Oh some young lady brought it personally by hand, not long after you left yesterday.'

'I want the video from the front office, now. I need to see who brought it in,' Alan said with some urgency. 'Now!' he shouted at Frank.

Twenty minutes later Frank arrived back with the video and they began viewing it together.

'Are we having a briefing today, boss?' one of the lads enquired.

'Not now, I'll call one later. Tell everyone to stay on the air,' Alan replied.

'All I can say boss is, you'll know this woman when you see her, she's very attractive,' Frank stated.

'Frank why are we looking at it all? I left the office at 3.30 p.m. Go from there.'

Butcher fast forwarded the video and then began viewing it again.

'There she is.' Frank pressed the pause button.

'Who the fuck's that?' Alan asked.

Frank just shrugged his shoulders and said, 'She refused to give her name. I thought she must have known you.'

'I need that girl!' Alan stated.

'Don't we all, boss,' Frank replied.

'On your list of SAS members, does the name Christopher Parker appear?'

'I don't know boss, I'll go and have a look.' Frank left the office and returned with the list.

'Yes boss, he was chucked out of the SAS, having gained the rank of Major.'

'Fucking hell,' Alan muttered and looked at the list given to him by Butcher.

'Does that name appear on the Hilton Hotel guest list Frank?'

'We don't have it yet Sir.'

'I want that list now, do you hear.'

'Yes boss I'll get on to it right away.'

Butcher left the office, he glanced back watching Alan browsing at the list of names.

'What's up Frank?' one of the lads shouted.

'Don't know but the boss must be on to something.'

Alan arranged a meeting with the Chief, and left the office

shortly afterwards. On leaving he asked Frank to contact him as soon as he had the list from the Hotel.

On meeting the Chief, Alan handed him the envelope and said, 'I'm not going to say a word until you've read that.'

The Chief sat down and commenced to read the package, his secretary entered the room and handed both of them a cup of tea.

Half an hour later the Chief looked at Alan, 'You're joking?'

'I don't know Sir, it's so far-fetched I know, it could be true.'

'What do we know that could back it up?' the Chief enquired.

Alan then explained that it was a good reason for General Winters being difficult and the link with the army equipment. 'Parker was in the SAS and I understand Winters has some kind of operation on, later today at the Hilton,' Alan finished.

'What about Lomax?' the Chief added.

'Well fortunately Sir, he's your problem and quite frankly if the information is right, he put all this together.'

As the discussion went on, Alan's mobile phone rang. 'Excuse me sir.' He answered it.

'Butcher, Sir. I have the list from the Hilton.'

'Does Parker ...?' but Alan was interrupted by Butcher saying, 'Yes Sir, Parker is in room 405.'

Alan instructed Butcher to get the team together and to obtain a plan of the Hilton Hotel and surrounding area.

Alan informed the Chief, 'Well Sir, it would appear as if our Major Parker is staying at the Hilton Hotel.'

The Chief shouted to his secretary, and she entered the office. 'I'm going to the incident room. I require the Tactical Firearms Inspector to see me straight away. He'll need a firearms team ready, I'll authorise the firearms issue.'

She left the office and when leaving the office himself, Alan saw that she was already on the telephone to the Firearms Department.

'Alan?'

'Yes Sir.'

The Chief handed back the envelope. 'This has to be kept under lock and key, Let's get Parker and we'll sort Lomax later.'

'I didn't think you would want anyone else to know at this stage,' Alan whispered.

'Not yet, his time will come.'

It was nearing twelve noon and the Chief, Alan and Butcher had a meeting with Inspector Eastwood, the On-Duty Firearms expert.

All four spent the next half-hour studying plans of the Hotel and the surrounding road layout.

'Right,' said the Chief. 'When can we get this up and running?'

'About two hours Sir. We will need to know if our suspect is in his room or not,' Eastwood replied.

The Chief looked at his watch, 'OK two thirty then, but Alan I need some of your boys to watch the Hotel.'

'No problem Sir.'

Alan and the Chief attended a briefing with the team and brought them up to speed with the day's events.

Two teams were sent to the hotel to see if they could locate Parker.

At 1 p.m. the telephone rang in room 405 at the Hilton.

Parker answered it, 'Yes?'

'Evans here, we'll meet at 3 p.m. multi-story car park, Cannon Street, don't be late,' and the phone went dead before Parker could reply.

Parker checked his handgun and placed a box of spare rounds into his jacket pocket. He then left the room. He wanted to get to the meeting point early to review the car park. He already knew that Evans would have done the same.

As Parker left the hotel, two Ford Mondeo motor cars pulled

up in front of the hotel, and eight plainclothes Police Officers got out and made their way to the hotel foyer.

The Chief anxiously waited in the office as he watched the minutes of the clock tick by to 2.25 p.m.

Alan was at the scene in company with Inspector Eastwood.

'Have we had confirmation Sir?' Eastwood enquired.

'No, we've been unable to confirm the suspect's whereabouts,' Alan replied.

'Do you wish us to go, Sir?' Eastwood asked.

'Yes, as arranged,' Alan instructed.

At precisely 2.30 p.m. Inspector Eastwood spoke into his radio 'Go. Go. Go.'

On hearing this, the Firearms Team sprang into action; two officers dressed in ballistic overalls used a 'ram-it' on the door of room 405, which caused it to burst from its hinges.

Before the door landed on the floor, other officers ran into the room shouting, 'Armed Police'. They found the room empty.

Alan entered the room, had a casual look round, and then instructed Butcher to get forensics to give it a good going over.

Alan left the room, stood the Firearms Team down and used his mobile phone to ring the Chief. 'He's gone Sir, I'll be back in the office shortly.'

Alan told Eastwood to be on standby with his team, 'I'll keep the hotel under observation, you never know he might return.'

Alan returned to the office and had lengthy discussions with the Chief about their next course of action. They agreed to speak to the Commissioner later that day.

Butcher returned to the office and met with Alan.

'We could find nothing of real value, the staff gave a description which would fit Parker. Oh yes, Parker did receive two telephone calls. One from a bed and breakfast, and one from a call box in Cannon Street.'

'What arrangements have you made to keep the room under

observations, Frank?' Alan enquired.

'I've left two teams, each have a Firearms Officer with them,' Frank replied.

Butcher had just returned to the office when he received a telephone call from Peter Mann.

'Hello Pete.'

'Your man has gone to the Cannon Street multi story, Winters is already en route. It's shoot to kill. See you later Frank.' The phone went dead.

Frank rushed from his seat, 'Boss.'

'What the hell's the matter, Frank?'

'Winters is at the Cannon Street carpark, it's Parker and the instructions are shoot to kill.'

'Are you sure?' Alan enquired.

'It's the informant I told you about yesterday.'

Alan turned to the Chief, 'It'll be right Sir, and Parker did get that call from a phone box in Cannon Street.'

The Chief instructed Eastwood to attend at the car park with his firearms team. Alan left with the Chief. The whole area around New Scotland Yard exploded with the sound of two-tone sirens.

Whilst rushing through the streets Alan thought to himself, 'God, I hope we're not too late. Winters will have only one thing in his mind – to eliminate his problem.'

Parker attended the fourth floor of the multi story carpark and could hear footsteps coming from one of the stairwells. Suddenly the door flung open, his heart missed a beat, he didn't know what Evans had intended.

Standing in front of him was Evans, still limping from his leg injury.

'God, I'm glad to see you,' Parker said as he looked down at Evans' leg.

'That's what you did, you bastard.'

'It had nothing to do with me, I swear,' Parker was failing in trying to convince Evans.

Evans shouted, 'I'm going to kill you, bastard!' and produced a handgun from his pocket. Almost simultaneously Parker produced a handgun. Both held the weapons against each other's head. 'Where do we go from here then?' Parker asked.

'Why, why did you have to kill them?'

Parker again pleaded his innocence. 'It had nothing to do with me. Let's just split the proceeds of the job and get out of here.'

Evans said, 'It's not as simple as that, someone has to pay for the boys, if not you, who did it?' His voice rose as he shouted 'Who?'

In the distance two shadowy figures were lying in wait, high on the rooftops of nearby buildings.

'Falcon one, in position, clear view.'

General Winters was sitting inside a van with blacked out windows; it was parked in Cannon Street. Unusually for the time of day, nothing else was moving in the area.

'Falcon two, in position, clear view.'

Winters listened to the radio as both of his men stated they were ready to proceed with the operation.

'Sir, the men are ready for your orders,' the operation commander turned his head towards Winters. 'Sir?'

Winters paused for a moment, then looked towards the commander and quietly said, 'OK get on with it.'

The Commander then instructed his men 'Falcon one, Falcon two it's a go, go.'

Both men without question raised sniper rifles and began focusing in on their targets.

'Come on man, give it up,' Parker pleaded.

At that moment both Evans and Parker could hear footsteps coming up the stairs. The door of the fourth floor landing opened and an elderly female with a young child appeared. The sight startled her, seeing two grown men, pointing guns at each other's head. She screamed, pulled the child away and ran out through the door, from where she had just come.

'Falcon one, civilian targets appeared, female and child.'

'Falcon two, I confirm.'

The commander turned to Winters, 'Sir?'

Winters coldly stared at the Commander, 'Carry on.'

'Yes sir, Falcon one, Falcon two, instructions it's a go, go.'

'Falcon one, confirm.'

'Falcon two, confirm.'

Parker and Evans could hear the sound of a child crying in the background.

' What are we going to do?' Parker asked Evans.

At that point, small red dots appeared on Parker's and Evans' forehead.

As the red dots appeared Parker said, 'It would appear as if we are not alone.'

Evans acknowledged, 'You as well.'

Almost at the same time police cars appeared in Cannon Street.

As his vehicle entered Cannon Street Alan saw the van with blacked out windows. 'Driver over there, to that vehicle, the black van.' He knew that was where he would find Winters.

Police vehicles screeched to a halt all round the carpark and armed Police Officers got out of the vehicles and took up vantage positions.

Alan jumped out of the police car and ran over to the van, shouting, 'Winters – call it off.'

'Falcon one, await instructions, target in sight.'

'Falcon two, confirm, target in sight.'

'Winters?' Alan shouted.

'Falcon one, target sighted, await instructions.'

'Falcon two, confirmed target sighted.'

The two SAS Commandos gently squeezed the trigger of the high velocity rifles as they waited for the fatal call to kill their targets.

Alan MacKenzie in rage opened the van door and shouted, 'I'll have you for murder Winters, I warn you.'

'Falcon one, any instructions?'

'Sir?' the commander shouted.

Winters looked at Alan and knew that he wasn't bluffing. 'Commander abort the mission.'

'Falcon one, abort, repeat abort mission.'

'Falcon one received.'

'Falcon two, abort, repeat abort mission.'

'Falcon two received.'

On receiving the instructions the two SAS Commandos left their posts, and disappeared.

'I only hope you know what you're doing MacKenzie.'

'I'm just glad I'm not arresting you for murder at this time,' Alan replied.

Parker wasted no time, he noticed the red dot on Evans' forehead had disappeared, he pulled the trigger of his handgun and felt his arm jolt back and saw Evans fall to the ground, his body lifeless.

'No,' Alan shouted as he heard the sound of a gunshot.

He looked at Winters and shouted, 'You're not going anywhere.' He ordered one of the Firearm Officers to ensure that Winters did not move, if he did he was to be arrested for conspiracy to murder.

'It's not my men,' Winters said, 'go and play your stupid games, policeman.'

Parker had noticed that when the woman and child appeared, she dropped a set of car keys near to a Ford Escort motor car.

He ran over to it, picked the keys up, tried them in the lock. The door opened and he got into the vehicle.

Parker paused for a moment and knew from his reconnaissance of the area prior to the meeting Evans that there was a way out. He started the engine up and screeched the car into motion. The Firearms Team heard the commotion and took up position at the exit point of the car park and raised their firearms, waiting for Parker's vehicle to appear. As they waited the woman and child appeared and began to walk across the entrance.

The screeching of tyres got louder as it approached the entrance. Police Officers began to shout at them to get out of the way. The woman became more frightened and clung onto the child; she froze, rooted to the spot.

Suddenly her red Ford motor car appeared racing towards her, A Police Officer ran towards her and just managed to pull her and the child out of the way as the car reached the spot where she was standing. A number of gunshots rang out, the windscreen of the vehicle shattered. The vehicle continued to race by the officers standing outside in Cannon Street.

The officers failed to notice due to the excitement of the woman and child being in the way, Parker had opened the driver's door and jumped out of the vehicle, rolling away out of sight. The red Escort careered out of control as the Police Officers continued to fire shots into it. It collided into a stationary police car and immediately burst into flames.

MacKenzie appeared at the scene, he raised his hands to his head and shouted, 'Fuck it!'

The Firearm Team surrounded the vehicle in case anyone moved from it. A secondary explosion occurred as the car petrol tank exploded. Within minutes the Fire Brigade attended the scene, as did an ambulance.

MacKenzie was back at his car talking with the Chief when

he was informed that there was no one in the vehicle. It was empty. Alan immediately instructed the Firearms Teams to conduct a thorough search of the car park. The woman and child were taken away by ambulance to hospital, suffering from shock.

Alan turned to Winters, 'You, you bastard, get out of my sight, I'll have you for perverting the course of justice.'

'You could never make it stick,' Winters replied as he instructed his driver to move off.

Five hours later a full search of the carpark had been completed. Parker had made good his escape. It was then closed to the public as the Forensic Officers commenced gathering evidence from the scene where Evans' body was found. The Ford Escort was taken away for detailed examination.

MacKenzie left instructions that once the scene had been cleared they would have a debriefing. Alan and the Chief returned to the office. The debrief showed that Parker had escaped via a drainage duct, which led into a nearby street. The identity of Evans was also now known, as Winters had been instructed to assist the police fully with their enquiries.

The Chief had agreed with Alan that Parker's photograph would have to be publicised on national television. He arranged to do that later that evening. Because the meeting with the Commissioner had been cancelled it was also agreed that the two of them should meet with the Commissioner first thing in the morning to discuss the contents of the envelope.

Alan was about to leave for the television studio when Frank Butcher said, 'He's a callous bastard, Parker, isn't he?'

'Very much so,' Alan replied, 'but there's more to this story than you think. We'll get him.' He patted Frank on the back, 'Come on, let's get off.'

Alan appeared on the nine o'clock news and launched his appeal for information, which could lead to he arrest of Parker.

Parker's photograph appeared on every television station and in every newspaper from then on. Alan returned to his Hendon room that night exhausted. He lay on his bed and quickly fell asleep.

At 8 a.m. he was awoken by the mobile phone ringing. 'Hi darling,' he said.

'Are you alright?' Helen enquired.

Alan then informed her of the day he had before and that it was going to be busy for the next few days as things had developed.

'I know you are busy, but if we could get together soon, it'll be nice, bye.'

The mobile went dead. Alan looked at his watch and thought, 'I'm going to be late, this is getting to be a habit.'

He washed, dressed and arrived at work just before 9 a.m. ready for the briefing. Alan was quite surprised by the arrival of the Commissioner, who had arrived with the Chief Constable for the briefing.

The briefing was a little less jovial than normal, whether it was because the Commissioner was there or that the team was getting tired, Alan didn't know. The briefing was told that no telephone calls had been received since the television broadcast. Alan stated, 'We can only assume from this, that Parker has gone to ground.'

The briefing ended and the Chief, the Commissioner and Alan went into his office. Alan unlocked his desk drawer and removed a brown envelope from it. The Chief took hold of it and asked the Commissioner to read its contents, which he did.

On completion the Commissioner said, 'Well?'

This took Alan and the Chief quite by surprise.

Alan broke the momentary silence saying, 'The contents could be correct.'

'What have we got to back this theory up?' the Commissioner enquired.

'Circumstantial only,' the Chief replied.

'What do you want me to do?' the Commissioner asked.

'Well we need to get Parker first, in order to progress Lomax,' replied Alan.

'It's the political aspect, Sir, which is a concern,' the Chief then remarked.

'When the time comes, I'll have to sort that out, will I not?' the Commissioner stated. 'Until then I suggest you keep this matter under wraps, and concentrate on getting this Parker, preferably alive. It's the only way he's going to answer questions.'

The Chief and Alan in unison replied, 'Yes Sir.'

The Commissioner then left the office, 'Keep me informed.'

Alan and the Chief looked at each other in amazement.

'Well he took that pretty lightly,' the Chief said.

Alan instructed Frank to keep the hotel room under observation in case Parker was daft enough to return.

CHAPTER TWELVE

Parker had finally decided that time had come for him to leave the country. He knew that the millions he had made were safe and that he had enough money in his bank account to see him through the next few months. He contacted Heathrow airport and arranged a flight on the 11.30 plane leaving for Vancouver.

At 09.30 hours he left the Regency Hotel bound for Heathrow. He decided that it had been too risky to return to the Hilton. He boarded the underground train. As he passed through the station terminal he noticed a young Police Officer.

Police Constable 987 Martin Staines had only been with the Transport Police for eight months. His day began just as any other, and as he had the daily briefing his mates joked about the most wanted man in Britain. Martin had suffered many taunts from his senior colleagues, but being the probationer it was the norm. He passed the jokes off by saying, 'I wish I could find him, it'll put your noses out of joint.' The room filled with laughter as one of the senior colleagues replied 'You'll piss your pants if you came across him.'

Martin went out on patrol as usual, passing general pleasantries as people passed by. Suddenly he felt the hairs stand up on the back of his neck. He glanced across the station reception area and there saw a figure of a man, who he thought he recognised.

Martin paused for thought as the man passed through the terminal, losing sight of him.

'Bloody hell,' he shouted to himself, causing members of the public stood by him, to look up, saying, 'Excuse me'.

Martin looked up and scanned the area to see if he could see the man. At the bottom of the escalator he saw the same man he had seen earlier getting off the moving platform as it met the lower level.

Martin couldn't make out the features of the man to confirm his suspicions so he began to make his way down the escalator. As he did so he pulled a folded piece of paper from out of his tunic pocket and unravelled it. The piece of paper had the photograph of Parker on it. They had just been delivered to the parade room prior to him going out on patrol. He thought himself fortunate to have bothered picking the paper up. He decided that before making himself the subject of ridicule, he would check that the man was the same as that in the photograph.

Parker, as he stepped off the escalator, glanced at his watch. He had decided that he would time it so that he would reach Heathrow an hour before his flight.

On entering the station terminal he had seen the young policeman, and as he stepped onto the lower level he looked back and saw the officer following him. As Parker reached the platform a tube train was just pulling up, the doors opened and Parker pushed his way onto the train before the passengers waiting to get off had disembarked. He waited by the doors.

Martin Staines stepped onto the lower level and as he did so he accidentally knocked into a female commuter causing her to drop her bags. He stopped to assist her to pick them up, trying to apologise for his clumsiness. As he entered the platform the stationary train was about to move off. As the doors began to close he noticed a man suddenly get off the train towards the front.

Parker had timed things badly, he had assumed that the young constable had managed to get onto the train. As a result of him getting onto the train near to the front, he had found himself in a position where he couldn't see the Police Officer arriving on the platform. He found himself getting off the train just as the young PC had arrived.

Parker put his head down and tried to look inconspicuous and began walking towards the officer. When only a matter of feet away Martin asked for Parker to stop.

'Yes Officer, can I help you?' Parker enquired.

'Can you tell me where you are going Sir?'

Parker paused, 'I'm trying to get a train to the airport, I somehow managed to get onto the wrong train.'

'Do you mind giving me your name please?' the officer demanded.

'Not at all Officer, Paul Templeton,' Parker stated.

'Have you got some form of identification on you?'

At that point Parker struck the officer a blow to the base of his neck causing him to fall to the ground. Parker ran off. Members of the public rushed to Martin's assistance and helped him onto his feet. He looked up and saw Parker running up the escalator, on reaching the top Parker glanced back.

Martin was certain the photograph and the man were one and the same person. He commenced to follow Parker and radioed for assistance. When he reached the top of the escalator he scanned the station terminal but could see no sign of Parker. He began to panic, and at that moment began to feel the pain to his neck where Parker had given the blow, 'Shit,' he muttered to himself as he rubbed the spot on his neck, realising at the same time he had lost his man.

The assistance call was met with a little apprehension from his colleagues, thinking that maybe PC Staines was taking the Mickey out of them, following the earlier conversation at the briefing.

Still rubbing his neck Martin turned and glanced up the

escalator where he again saw Parker; he had doubled back and taken his coat off. Martin again called for assistance.

The radio operator replied to the call, 'Are you sure it's the wanted person Parker?'

Martin in frustration shouted back, 'Yes'.

Parker had reached the platform. As he did another train pulled into the station and he got on. Martin this time reached the train as the doors were closing and managed to scramble on board. As the train pulled away from the station Martin checked the platform to see if his man had got off the train. He was certain he was still on the train.

Martin started to make his way forward on the train, checking every passenger as he went. He felt apprehensive and felt his hand shake on the back of the passenger seats as he held on while the train shunted from side to side. He began to get nervous.

The train began to come to a stop. Parker got off and began to run to the exit. Passengers getting off the train held up Martin. Parker left the station and got into a black cab at the entrance. Martin had just reached the entrance when he saw the taxi pulling away. Parker looked out of the back window to see the young constable, standing out of breath staring back at him.

Martin updated the radio operator and flagged down another black cab. 'Follow that cab,' he shouted.

The taxi driver turned round and said, 'Is this for real mate?'

Angrily Martin gave the cabby a stern look and shouted, 'Yes.'

The taxi driver managed to keep Parker's taxi in sight until it reached Heathrow airport, where he lost it in the mêlée of black cabs.

Martin radioed his location, where he was told to stand by for assistance.

* * *

MacKenzie was sat at his desk when the office door flung open. 'We had a good sighting, Sir,' Butcher announced.

'Whereabouts?' Alan asked.

'A young PC spotted him on the underground and followed him to Heathrow,' Butcher replied.

Alan grabbed his coat and rushed out of the office with Frank.

'Have you got the area well covered, Frank?' Alan asked.

'Yes boss, the airport police are sealing the area off and the rest of the team are on the way.'

'Good.' Alan paused, 'Good'.

There was a deathly silence in the car as it reached Heathrow. Alan was worried that he was about to lose his man.

Parker had by now collected his ticket and entered the departure lounge, he bought a paper and opened it, holding it high to cover his face. His plane was on time and his heart was racing, hoping that he could get on it before the airport was searched. He had twenty minutes to wait. Every minute seemed like an hour to him.

Alan MacKenzie met young Police Officer Staines, 'How sure are you it's the right man, son?' he asked.

'I've got this photograph of him Sir, I'm one hundred per cent Sir, it was him,' Martin stuttered a little as he gave Alan confirmation of the sighting.

Alan was informed by airport security that the police would be unable to cancel any flights or even delay any. He knew that he only had one chance of finding Parker. If he got onto his plane it would take years to get him, if at all. The team began a search of the airport terminals.

'Last calls for the 11.30 flight to Vancouver, now boarding at gate 24.'

Parker heard the female's voice over the tannoy. He got up

from his seat, glanced around and followed the rest of the passengers for the flight out of the terminal doors and boarded the bus, which was to take him to the plane. The bus conveyed the passengers to the rear of the aircraft and they began to get off. As Parker got off the bus he looked back at the terminal to see if any Police Officers were following.

Martin felt the hairs stand up on the back of his neck again, as on instinct he looked out of the terminal windows and there saw Parker, looking right back at him. Martin jumped back behind a concrete pillar hoping that Parker hadn't seen him.

Parker turned and began to step onto the stairs leading to the aeroplane. At the top of the stairs he again stopped and looked back. He couldn't see the young Police Officer and entered the plane. Once on the plane he thought he was home and safe. He had not lost sight of the fact if he had been seen there was no way he could escape.

Martin Staines began sweating and looked around frantically for Alan MacKenzie. He eventually found him.

'Sir, Sir, I've seen him,' he said panting and out of breath.

'Whereabouts?' Alan enquired with urgency in his voice.

Martin pointed out the aircraft just as the stairs were being removed from it.

Alan enquired which flight the aircraft was and how he could stop it. He was told that the flight was to Vancouver and he would be unable to stop it.

'To hell with that,' he shouted and made his way out onto the aircraft reception area.

'Come on son!' he shouted to Martin.

He stopped one of the stewards and stated that he wanted the aircraft stopping.

'No chance mate, you're too late,' the steward said.

Butcher glanced round to see Alan running out of the terminal with the young constable. He instinctively knew Alan was onto something so followed in that direction.

Alan grabbed hold of the steward and pulled him towards an airport vehicle parked nearby. They got into the vehicle and Alan started to drive the vehicle towards the runway.

'Are you bloody mad?' the steward shouted.

'I want that plane stopping.'

'You can't,' the steward stated.

'Watch me,' Alan replied.

The aircraft had just reached the end of the runway and was beginning to take off.

Parker knew he was safe once the aircraft engines began to rev up. 'Good morning ladies and gentlemen we are about to take off, may I wish you a happy journey on behalf of Britannia Airways.'

Parker listened to the pilot as the noise of the engines began to become deafening. He smiled, as he knew he was now safe.

The aircraft began to move. Suddenly it came to an abrupt halt. Parker looked out of the window. He couldn't see anything. He knew there was nowhere to go. The runway was blocked and air traffic was being diverted to Stansted.

After twenty minutes the door to the aircraft opened and Chief Inspector Alan Duncan MacKenzie climbed on board, in company with Police Constable Martin Staines. Alan walked down the isle of the plane checking each passenger in turn. When he reached Parker's seat he said.

'Mr Parker, we meet again.'

Parker looked at MacKenzie; he smiled then offered MacKenzie both hands, expecting him to place handcuffs onto him.

'No Parker, there's nowhere for you to go.'

Alan turned to the young constable and said, 'What did you say your name was son?'

'Martin Staines, Sir.'

'Well Martin, this is certainly going to leave a stain on you for the rest of your career. You can arrest this man for murder,' Alan winked at Martin.

Without hesitating PC Staines turned to Parker. 'I am arresting you for the offence of murder, you do not have to say anything but it may harm your defence if you do not mention when questioned something which you may later rely on in court, anything you say may be given in evidence.'

Parker looked at Alan and said, 'You did well Mr Policeman, you have a long way to go yet.'

Parker was led to the top of the stairway; he paused and looked around. Police vehicles surrounded the aircraft and armed Police Officers had their sights pointed on the plane. Parker looked at Alan, turned and began walking down the stairs towards uniformed officers, who placed handcuffs on him and took him to a nearby police van.

CHAPTER THIRTEEN

Later that evening Alan's mobile telephone rang, it was Helen. 'Hi' he said in a rather excited voice.

'I've heard on the news, is it true, you've got him?'

'Yes darling, it's him,' Alan said.

'Any chance of seeing you later?' She waited in anticipation for the reply.

'Do you know, that's just what I could do with. Yes all right, shall I pick you up, about 9.30?'

'That'll be lovely,' she replied.

Frank Butcher returned to Alan's office. 'How's the interview going, Frank?' Alan enquired.

'Not too well, he keeps asking to speak to you, he won't talk to any one else.'

'I'll leave it until the morning, if nothing happens by then, I'll speak to him.'

'OK, boss,' Frank replied.

Alan left the office feeling quite elated over the arrest of Parker, but he knew however that there might be bigger fish to fry. He also knew that Parker was the key to the next stage of the enquiry, He was glad to get away from the office as he was getting fed up with people ringing him up, congratulating him on his arrest.

He chuckled to himself as he thought that the crime of the century was again solved by a young police constable doing good old-fashioned police work. He chuckled louder when he thought how close it came to losing the biggest mass murderer this century.

Alan arrived at his Hendon room where he packed his bag, paid his outstanding bill and left very quickly, returning to his own home. As he opened the flat door he found a pile of letters on the doorstep which had accumulated since his hasty departure following Parker's untimely appearance.

Alan again chuckled to himself, thinking of Helen and himself being found in such a compromising condition by two female officers, and again chuckled, even louder, as he visualised Helen's face that morning. Alan dumped the pile of letters on the tabletop, then poured himself a glass of whisky and gently sipped from the glass. 'How nice it is to be back in your own home,' he thought to himself.

He walked over to the window to gaze out on to the busy streets of London. He could see his reflection in the glass and he thought to himself, how he had aged.

He held his glass up high and saluted, 'To you up there, thank you.' He placed the glass to his lips and in one gulp swallowed the remaining contents of the glass.

He showered, dressed and left the flat just before 9 p.m. arriving at Helen's at 9.25 p.m.

On answering the door, she stood momentarily looking at the man she loved, then without any further hesitation hugged him tight. 'You must be exhausted,' she whispered in his ear.

'No, I'm alright, now I've seen you. What do you want to do, stay in or eat out?'

Helen looked at Alan again, 'We'll go out for something to eat, then back here, I want you to stay the night.'

'Without interruptions I hope,' Alan winked at her and smiled, 'Let's hope so,' she muttered.

She grabbed her coat and said, 'Come on'.

Helen and Alan returned to her house at a round 11 p.m. and she poured them both a glass of whisky. She looked at Alan, 'Come on, time for some therapy.'

Alan followed into the bedroom where he gazed at Helen as she undressed. She moved towards him and gently kissed him, as she gently ran her finger down his front, reaching his belt buckle. She started to unfasten it as Alan began to remove his shirt.

'Darling,' he muttered, as she touched his manhood. He moved towards her and gently pushed her back onto the bed, where he began to caress her lips, her face, and shoulder, then began moving slowly down her body kissing her nipples as he went. He moved his face across her stomach, which caused her whole body to raise with excitement. Alan gently moved his body back towards her and kissed her lips as he entered her. She gasped with pleasure as she whispered, 'Darling, I love you'.

The next morning Alan rose early, showered and made breakfast. At 8.30 a.m. he woke Helen. 'Good morning darling, I have to go,' he said as he passed the tray which had tea and toast perched on it, to Helen.

'This looks rather nice, I hope you're going to make a habit of this?' she said smiling.

'Too much of a good thing's bad for you, you know.' He looked at her, paused and said, 'I've got a busy day today, I don't know what time I'll get finished.'

'I'll see you when I see you then.' She paused as Alan began to walk away, 'Alan?'

Alan turned and looked at her.

'I love you.'

He smiled and walked away.

The morning briefing was a joyous one as everyone knew their man was in custody and they could relax for the first time in months.

After the Inspector updated the arrest day's events Alan brought the meeting to a close by saying, 'Gentlemen, it hasn't ended yet, there is a lot of work to do. How we go about it will affect a lot of people, even you will be surprised by the outcome.'

The Chief who had been at the briefing turned to Alan and said, 'What now?'

'Well Sir it would appear as if our man will not speak to anyone but me. I think it may be quite interesting, do you want to join me?'

'Erm, no I don't think so, I feel I had better remain impartial on this one.'

'Frank,' Alan shouted.

'Yes boss?'

'Come on then, interview.'

Frank Butcher was surprised when Alan asked him to go on the interview and asked, 'Why me boss?'

'I thought you were my right hand man.'

'I suppose so boss.'

'Well come on then, you can show me all about PACE interviewing, and putting questions into little boxes,' he laughed as he walked off towards the charge room.

CHAPTER FOURTEEN

The interview commenced. Frank placed the sealed tapes into the recording machine and began to introduce himself. He was about to ask Alan to introduce himself when Parker interrupted.

'I don't need this, turn the tapes off,' he shouted.

Alan informed Parker that official procedures had to be carried out and that he, Parker, should know this having served in the army.

Butcher continued with the opening procedures.

On completion Alan said, 'I understand that you wished to speak to me. My officers have interviewed you on several occasions, and on each of those occasions you have made the same request.'

Parker looked at Alan, 'Yes, that's right.'

'What do you want to say?'

Parker paused, 'Look, this is all shit, I have been employed by the Government to complete this operation. I cannot say anything further.'

Alan said, 'All I can say to you is that this is your opportunity to tell me what that task was and who authorised it.'

Parker again paused, 'I am unable to say.'

'Well I can only tell you that you have committed murder on a grand scale, you are not employed by any official government office, say the army for instance. I cannot see anyone in the Government authorising the slaughter of thousands of civilians in this country. It just would not happen.'

'Well it has,' Parker stated firmly.

'Mind you, it could explain why the SAS tried to kill you.'

Alan looked Parker straight into his eyes.

'What?'

'It was me who prevented Winters from giving the order to kill you,' Alan again waited for a reply from Parker.

'I thought that was the police.'

'No, it was the SAS, maybe someone was trying to cover his tracks. You were not meant to be sat here talking to me. Do you understand?' Alan raised his voice.

'Look I cannot say any more, I need to speak to the Home Secretary, Lomax.'

'Why?' Alan enquired.

There was no reply as Parker just stared at Alan.

Alan interrupted the silence saying, 'Well, all I can say is that you will not be speaking to anyone, you will be charged with murder. Unless you have some proof of what you are telling me is correct, I am not going to waste any more time if you're not going to tell me what I need to know. This is not the army.'

Alan rose from the table and indicated to Butcher to close the tapes.

Frank was just about to turn the tape off when Parker spoke, 'Wait.'

Alan calmly said, 'Did you want to speak?'

'This is a difficult situation for me, do you understand? I have never been in this position before, it's not like being in the army, you're right.'

'Parker you have no option but to tell me.'

'Can I trust you?'

'Parker, you're on your own here. I am willing to listen to you,' Alan paused.

There was a long pause in the interview room as Parker considered his options, then five minutes had passed.

'Well?' Alan said.

'OK, you saved my life, I'll tell you what you need to know.'

Butcher raised his eyebrow as Parker commenced to tell his story. Four hours later Alan suggested that they all had a break. Butcher closed the last of six sets of tapes.

Parker was led back to his cell, but as the door closed Alan turned to Butcher and said, 'Not a word to the team yet, as to the contents of the tapes.'

'Well Sir, I'm lost for words. I take it from your lack of surprise, you already knew?'

'Come back to the office and I'll fill you in with the details.' Frank looked slightly puzzled by this.

Word had already got back to the enquiry team that Parker was talking, and the team had gathered to see what had been said.

Alan instructed the team to take the rest of the day off and that he would give a full account in the morning's briefing.

An air of disappointment seeped through the room as Alan left.

Once in his office Alan instructed Butcher to close the door.

'Do you recall a young attractive female turning up with this?' Alan removed the brown envelope from his drawer and handed it to Butcher.

'Yes, I do.'

'Frank, read it.'

Alan picked up the telephone and rang the Chief Constable to update him on what Parker had said.

Frank was just about to conclude reading the contents of the envelope when he heard Alan telling the Chief that they would continue the interview with Parker that night. Alan replaced the phone.

'So you can see why I've been unable to tell you certain things?'

Frank looked at Alan, 'What makes me think that this is not an enquiry to be on?'

'Well Frank I thought the same, there are a lot of implications and a lot of decisions to be made by people greater than you or me, all we can do is our best.'

'Sir, why do you think a Home Secretary would do such a thing?'

'I don't know Frank, but he'll get his chance to tell us in due course. Let's get Parker sorted first.'

They both left the office to go to the custody suite.

After three hours of intensive interviewing, Alan decided that he had heard enough and began to wind up the interview.

On doing so Parker asked, 'What's going to happen to me?'

'Well, you will be charged with murder,' Alan replied.

'But I was employed by the Government, to do a job for them, I was only following instructions.' Parker placed his head into his hands and began to cry.

Alan was taken aback by the scene of such a man crying. He thought back to the time when he read Parker's personal file from the army. This was the man who wouldn't crack under torture.

'When will I be at court?'

Alan began to rise from his seat, 'Tomorrow.'

'Then what?'

'You will be remanded in to custody, until our enquiries are complete.'

'Chief Inspector, thank you for being honest with me.'

Alan paused and stared at Parker for a short while before leaving the interview room.

'Frank?'

'Yes boss.'

'Take Parker back to the cells please, I'll see you back in the office.'

Alan returned to the office and again telephoned the Chief Constable to inform him of the outcome of the interviews.

'I almost feel sorry for him you know,' Alan said to the Chief as he ended the conversation.

'Do you, why?'

'He has it in mind that he was working for the Government. He didn't realise that it was some personal thing which Lomax had dreamed up.'

'Anyway Alan, I'll be at the briefing in the morning, are you having him charged tonight?'

'Yes.'

'OK,' the telephone went dead.

Alan returned to his office and picked up a mug of hot tea and cupped it in both hands and began gently sipping at it. His thoughts were interrupted when Frank burst into Alan's office.

'Is that one for me?' pointing to a second mug of tea sat on the table top.

Alan nodded in acknowledgement

'You OK boss?'

'Yes, I've just been thinking, what was behind Lomax's thinking, what sparked all this off?'

'I wouldn't think about things like that boss, you'll come up with all the wrong answers,' Frank replied as he gulped down the now cool contents of his mug.

Another hour went by as Frank put the finishing touches to the charge sheets.

'Are you going to charge him, boss?'

Alan looked at Frank and said, 'No, I've become more involved that I should already by doing the interviews. You do it, you've done a good job on this case.'

'Are you coming to the charge room, boss?'

Alan sternly replied, 'No.'

Frank Butcher returned to the custody suite. Parker stood before him.

'Christopher Parker, I must tell you that you do not have to say anything but it may harm your defence if to do not mention now, something which you may later rely on in court, anything you say may be given in evidence. You are being charged that you did murder Paul Evans, an offence contrary to Common Law.'

Parker stood to attention and in regimental style replied, 'Yes Sir.'

Frank then placed further specimen charges on Parker relating to the deaths of his accomplices in Norfolk and one of the many thousands of people who had died by the lethal drugs, conspiracy to murder and drug offences.

On each occasion Parker sharply and clearly replied 'Yes Sir'.

CHAPTER FIFTEEN

At nine a.m. exactly the Chief Constable and Alan entered the briefing room. As Alan was about to commence the briefing, the Commissioner entered the room.

Alan gave a full account of the contents of the interviews to the gathering and indicated that there was evidence against the Home Secretary, Lomax, for conspiracy to murder.

There was a deathly silence in the briefing room as Alan related circumstances of Lomax's involvement. This was the first time, as a whole, that the team learned that Alan MacKenzie had been keeping things back from them. Looks of disbelief could be seen on many faces around the room.

At that point the Commissioner began to speak, 'As you can imagine, ladies and gentlemen, this has great implications to the Government. I am instructing you all that until this matter is sorted nothing will be said outside this room by anyone. I hope you all understand what I am saying?'

Alan then agreed with the Commissioner and said, 'Anyone found committing a breach of confidence will be dealt with severely.'

The briefing finished at 11.30 a.m. Alan, the Commissioner and the Chief retired to Alan's office to discuss the next move.

'Well Sir, I think that we should not delay the arrest of Lomax any further,' Alan said quietly.

The Commissioner agreed saying, 'We will however have to speak to the Prime Minister before we take any further action.'

'Is that wise Sir?' Alan enquired.

'I don't think we have any real options on that, because I feel that the implications to this whole matter will be far-reaching. Politics, who'll have them?' the Commissioner grunted.

The Commissioner picked up the telephone and dialled Number 10 Downing Street. He spoke directly to Maxwell.

'Yes Sir, we'll see you right away.' The Commissioner replaced the telephone.

'Right, come on then let's get this over and done with.'

Alan and the Chief accompanied the Commissioner out of the office.

'Frank?' Alan gestured him over, 'I want two teams standing by outside the Home Office and wait for my instructions.'

Frank nodded and went off in a hurry.

* * *

Maxwell was stunned by what he was told by the Commissioner. His face went visibly white as if every bit of blood in his body had been drained.

'Have we any other evidence against Lomax, other than what this Parker has indicated?' Maxwell enquired.

'Yes,' the Commissioner replied and requested Alan to hand over the contents of the brown envelope.

Maxwell spent the next half-hour digesting the report written by Lomax. 'And this is proof?' Maxwell asked.

Alan replied, 'Now we have the jigsaw pieces. Once Lomax is in custody we can firm up on the evidence side, Sir. There are other people who can firm matters up but we have been unable to approach them until now.'

Maxwell interrupted, 'Until Lomax is in custody?'

'Yes Sir,' Alan stated abruptly.

Maxwell discussed the implications of what had happened

and stated that he would have to resign over the issue. The room went silent, as no one knew what to say.

Alan gave a throaty cough and said, 'Sir, we can't delay any longer.'

Maxwell replied, 'What? Yes of course. Commissioner, I wish to speak to him first.'

'Do I have any option but to let you, Sir?' The Commissioner stared at Maxwell, who looked physically stressed. There was no reply.

On leaving Downing Street Alan got onto his mobile phone and rang Frank. 'Are the teams ready?' he enquired.

Frank simply replied, 'Yes'.

The phone went dead and Frank Butcher knew full well that the car travelling to the Home Office with Maxwell was not a vehicle he would have wished to be in. The shiny black Rover motor car pulled to a halt outside the Home Office and all four occupants got out of it. Maxwell wasted no time in climbing the steps to the Home Office and entered the building. He walked straight to Lomax's office.

Helen was sat at her desk and was startled to see Maxwell appear in the room without an appointment. She was even more startled to see Alan, the Chief and the Commissioner standing next to him.

Alan was gob-smacked when he saw Helen. He knew that she worked in a Government Department, he did not know that she was Lomax's secretary, and had never enquired about which department she had worked for.

In moments certain facts suddenly flashed through his mind. He began putting the pieces of evidence together. The brown envelope, the office junior, the girl who Frank couldn't keep his eyes off. She was sitting near to Helen.

Maxwell shouted at Helen, 'Is he in?'

Before she could reply Maxwell just walked past her and opened the door to Lomax's office and disappeared inside, slamming the door behind him.

'Is everything alright?' Helen enquired.

Alan took her aside, 'I didn't know you worked for Lomax?'

'Well you never asked,' she replied.

What's happening?' she asked.

Alan stated, 'I think you know most of it already, things have started to happen and Lomax will be arrested.'

'What about me?' Helen asked.

'You're not involved in this are you?' A worried look came over Alan's face.

'What do you take me for?' she replied, almost shouting. 'Alan, how can you suggest ...?' before Helen could complete her sentence she could hear shouting coming from inside Lomax's office.

Lomax was shocked to see Maxwell enter his office unannounced and without any greetings. Maxwell gave Lomax it with both barrels.

'Do you realise what you have done?'

'What are you on about?' enquired Lomax.

'Don't give me that shit, I know all about Parker and your involvement with the drug deaths,' Maxwell was raging and red in the face with anger.

'Have you given any thought about the Party?'

'The police cannot link anything with me, you or the Party,' Lomax stated.

'Why?' Maxwell pleaded, 'Why?'

Lomax stated, 'You got what you asked for, results. Harsh, but it worked. I was going to tell you but you didn't want to know.'

Maxwell shook his head in disbelief, 'What on earth do you think you were thinking of?'

'Look it will be fine, there's no link to us,' Lomax tried to assure Maxwell.

'You're wrong. I've seen the report you wrote to Parker.'

Lomax looked shocked, 'What? Oh my god, Helen.'

'Yes, as ever, she was very efficient,' Maxwell raised his eyebrow. 'All you have succeeded in doing is bringing us all down with you. I'll have to resign. The buck stops here.'

Maxwell turned his back and began to walk to the door. He paused, turned towards Lomax and said, 'The police are here to take you away.' He shook his head then turned away.

Maxwell opened the door and left, slamming the door behind him. He looked at the three Police Officers and said, 'Gentlemen he's all yours.'

Maxwell began to leave the office and before doing so instructed the Commissioner to update him every two hours on what was going on.

'Oh, gentlemen, no press please, leave them to me.'

Maxwell then left.

'Alan, is there anything I can do?' Helen asked quietly.

'No, leave it to us now,' he took hold of Helen's hand squeezed it gently, 'I'll see you later.'

Alan got onto his mobile phone and requested his team to attend the office. Then all three of them entered Lomax's office. It was empty.

Alan returned. 'Helen where's he gone?''

'He must have used his rear door, he'll be going to his car.' she replied.

Alan again got onto his mobile phone and instructed his team to block all vehicle access to the building. The team immediately blocked off all vehicle access to the building. It was too late, Lomax had gone. The team had missed him by seconds.

Alan remained whilst a full search was made of Lomax's office and ensured documents were seized.

On leaving Alan looked at Helen, 'I'll speak to you later.'

He then looked at the office junior and said, 'I'll need to see you later as well.'

'What about?' she replied rudely.

Helen butted in, 'I'll tell you shortly, be quiet for now.'

Alan left the office thinking to himself that at last everything was falling into place.

'Boss?'

'Yes.'

'Have you seen this?'

Butcher handed over a Customs Excise Report from Commander Jones about the Drugs Operation. The document had been found in Lomax's bottom drawer.

'Frank?'

'Yes Sir?' Frank Butcher was standing nearby waiting for Alan's next instructions.

'I need another two teams to come with me to Lomax's home address while the search is completed here.'

Without further word Alan got into his car and drove off to Lomax's home. On his arrival Alan saw Lomax's car on the driveway. He waited until the rest of the team arrived and gestured that some of them to go to the rear of the house, in case Lomax decided to do another runner. Alan knocked on the door to the house.

Lorraine answered the door. Alan introduced himself and asked, 'Is your husband at home?'

She replied, 'Yes he's in his study, do come in.'

Lorraine showed Alan to the study, she knocked and opened the door. Suddenly she screamed.

Alan pushed by her and saw Lomax, lying face down on his desk, lifeless. Nearby was a tipped up glass and a bottle of pills. A letter had been neatly placed on the blotting pad on the desk with the name 'Chief Inspector MacKenzie' written on it.

Alan opened the letter and stood in silence as he read it.

Dear Mr MacKenzie

I wish to apologise to all the people I have wronged.

I am solely responsible for the actions undertaken by Parker as he followed my instructions to the letter. I devised a plan, which I thought, wrongly, would eliminate people who sponge from the society as a whole, and who commit a large proportion of crime in this country.

I praise you and your enquiry team for the professional way you have conducted the investigation. I understand that you have all the evidence you require to close your investigation. There is nothing more I can say except sorry. There is no such thing as a perfect crime.

The letter was signed, *The Right Honourable Paul Lomax MP.*

Alan carefully placed the letter into a clear plastic evidence bag and requested a full examination of the scene be conducted.

CHAPTER SIXTEEN

Alan returned home late that evening and as he travelled home he heard the news report on the car radio that the Home Secretary had been found dead and that early indications were that he was found with gunshot wounds to the head. The news report ended by saying that further details would be given as they came in.

Alan chuckled to himself, thinking that they had already got the story wrong, no doubt thinking it was some IRA hit. 'Little do they know what's round the corner,' he muttered. His mind went off wondering what announcement the Prime Minister would make. There was very little on the news about Parker as Lomax's death took up most of the airtime.

On entering his flat Alan poured himself a tumbler full of whisky. He could see the message recorded light flashing on his answer machine and his finger paused over the button as he decided to retrieve his mesages.

He looked up and stretched his neck, he knew that Helen would have left a message. He pressed the button. Sure enough the first recording was from Helen, as was the second, sixth and tenth. There were other messages from wellwishers.

Alan switched his television on for the news. Lomax's death was headline news. It showed press and photographers surrounding the normally quiet area where Lomax lived. The news report stated that 'The Prime Minister was unavailable for comment but will be making a press release tomorrow morning after he has had a meeting with the Queen. It is now understood that the Home Secretary committed suicide and that the police are not treating his death as suspicious, although a forensic examination of the scene is still being conducted.'

Alan sat up when the news reporter announced that some more news had just come in on the death of the Home Secretary. The reporter announced that members of the Police team investigating the recent mass drug deaths visited Lomax's home address earlier today. Police were unavailable for comment.

The news bulletin went on to say that a man had appeared in court earlier charged in connection with the drug deaths. Alan picked up the telephone and rang Helen.

She answered, 'Hi it's me.'

'Are you alright?' she asked.

Alan gave a deep sigh, 'No not really, it's been a bastard of a day.'

'I'm coming round.' Before Alan could reply the telephone went dead.

Twenty minutes later Helen arrived at the door, Alan let her in and they both stood in the living room looking at each other for what appeared an eternity before they grabbed each other embracing.

'Oh I'm sorry,' Alan whispered.

'Shhhh,' she replied, 'don't say anything.'

Helen took Alan by the hand and led him into the bedroom where she began to unbutton his shirt. 'Helen?' he whispered.

'Shhhh,' she breathed warm air into his ear, 'not a word,' as she kissed him and began to undo his belt buckle.

Alan couldn't resist any further as he began to undo her clothing. He twisted her over and lay on top of her. He stopped and looked into her eyes. 'Darling I love you.'

'I love you too.' Alan kissed her, and she held him tight as he entered her and made love to her.

The night seemed endless, and as Alan dressed to go to work he suggested to Helen that it might be better if she took the day off work.

'I can't do that, I realise that there will be a lot of press around and I will have to face up to it.'

'You know that you will have to be interviewed about your knowledge of what has happened, don't you?'

'Yes.'

Alan began to leave the bedroom. 'Alan?'

'Yes?'

'I love you,' she smiled. Alan winked back and said, 'I know.' He turned and walked out.

Alan arrived at work just before 8 a.m. As he arrived he found the Chief and Commissioner waiting for him.

'Sorry Sir, I didn't realise you would be here this morning.'

The Commissioner replied, 'Well unfortunately we have a press conference to do, after the Prime Minister's given his. We're all meeting at Downing Street, at 9 a.m.'

Alan looked at his watch, 'We had better get off then, Sir.'

On reaching Downing Street there was a scramble to get past the hundreds of press standing outside.

All three were shown into the Cabinet room. Alan was taken aback when he saw the size of the highly polished mahogany table; he looked around the room. Pure white walls surrounded him decorated with oil paintings of past Prime Ministers.

Shortly afterwards they were joined in the room by other members of the Cabinet, closely followed by the Prime Minister.

They all sat and the room went quiet as Maxwell related the facts behind Lomax's death. A feeling of disbelief could be felt around the room.

Maxwell ended by stating he was seeing the Queen to tender his resignation. Shouts of 'NO!' echoed around the table.

Maxwell stated that he had no option but to resign.

At 11 a.m. Maxwell met the Queen and tendered his resignation. He left Buckingham Palace an hour and a half later, returning to Downing Street at 1p.m.

Maxwell got out of his car and walked over to the awaiting press.

'Ladies and gentlemen today I have visited Her Majesty the Queen to tender my resignation. This is following the tragic death of the Home Secretary Paul Lomax. Paul sadly took his own life yesterday for reasons which over the next few months will become apparent, but for legal reasons I am unable to make further comment. I can say however that it is in relation to the recent police investigations into the deaths of many thousands of people who died by taking contaminated drugs. I have nothing further to add.'

Maxwell then left, ignoring a frenzy of questions from the press, and entered 10 Downing Street.

At 2 p.m. the Commissioner held the police press conference. The police statement was short and simply stated that a man had appeared before the magistrates' court charged in connection with the drugs death enquiry and that they were not looking for anyone else in connection with it. He stated that the Home Secretary Paul Lomax had featured in the enquiry but for legal reasons could not say anything further.

The police press conference ended just after five minutes later.

Alan returned to New Scotland Yard with the Commissioner and the Chief and held a briefing with the team to thank them for their efforts during the enquiry. As he stood up to leave the room the sound of applause echoed through the briefing hall.

Alan stopped turned to his audience, the clapping stopped and Alan simply said, 'Thank you.'

On leaving Alan stopped the Commissioner, 'Excuse me Sir, have you seen these?' Alan was holding a file, 'It's the latest crime figures. It would appear that crime is down 60–70 per cent across the board. Sad really when you think about it. Did Lomax have it right?'

Alan turned away and walked off.

'MacKenzie,' the Commissioner shouted, 'Well done.'

MacKenzie entered his office, closed the door. He opened the bottom desk drawer and removed a glass tumbler and a bottle of best scotch, poured himself a glass and gazed out of his window.

The End